Operation: Dead Drop

Slater Security, Book 1

Charissa Gracyk

Operation: Dead Drop

Published by Charissa Gracyk

© Copyright 2022 by Charissa Gracyk

Edits by Michelle Fewer

Cover by Monique Walton/ moniquewalton515@gmail.com

ISBN: 9798437839263

ASIN: B09W87CYJ5

It is not legal to reproduce, duplicate, or transmit any part of this document in either electronic means or in printed format. Recording of this publication is strictly prohibited and any storage of this document is not allowed unless with written permission from the publisher except for the use of brief quotations in a book review.

This book is a work of fiction. Any resemblance to persons, living or dead, or places, events or locations is purely coincidental.

This series is dedicated to all my girls! Stay strong and fierce. GIRL POWER!

Chapter One: Fallon

Glock 9mm pistol. *Check*. OTF Automatic knife. *Check*. Ammo. *Check*. Night Vision Goggles. *Check*.

After carefully and methodically packing all of my gear according to TSA regulations, I glance over at the case with my HK416. *Do I bring the assault rifle, too?* I debate back and forth for a moment and then realize I probably won't need any of this.

My current job requires me to escort a fashion model from New York to Los Angeles. I'm providing protection from a stalker, but said stalker has been laying low lately. Which makes my job easier, of course, but much more boring.

I thrive on excitement so not packing my HK416

is a bit of a disappointment. *Boo. Maybe next time.*

Working for Slater Security based here in San Diego is the best thing that could've happened to me after separating from the military. It's a private firm that specializes in protection, defense and surveillance– among other more clandestine things. Which makes it right up my alley. My boss, Dash Slater, is former Delta Force and an all-around badass. Even though the ladies trip all over him because they can't get enough of his sharp cheekbones and baby blues, I see past his looks. I know and respect the real man. I've seen him in action and we've been stuck in some of the worst hellholes on Earth together.

Dash was my former commander and spent 15 years leading a tier-one counterterrorism unit, specifically directed to kill or capture high-value units or dismantle terrorist cells. He was damn good at his job and I learned a lot from him. We saved each other's skins more times than I care to count. Just as important, he treated me like an equal. As a woman in a Special Forces position that meant everything.

I knew when I was 16 that I wanted to join the military the moment I turned 18. My goal was to learn how to protect myself and others however I could. Learning how to shoot a gun was only a small part of my training. So much of it was mental. Especially when I encountered men who didn't think I belonged in a combat zone.

And I'm not just talking about the enemy.

Working my way through the ranks and endless Army training, I proved that I was one of the best. My eyes and mind were set on 1st Special Forces Operational Detachment-Delta, better known as Delta Force. It hasn't even been ten years since the DOD opened all combat positions across the military to women, completely lifting gender restrictions. Several women have passed Special Forces Assessment and Selection (SFAS) and I am damn proud to be in that minority.

Delta Force, also known as CAG (Combat Applications Group) or Task Force Green, was the hardest job I ever had and I loved the challenges. Our missions were super secretive and the shadowy world we moved in kept my pulse pounding. Calling myself an adrenaline junkie is an understatement. I was the perfect candidate and a master at the dark arts of counter terrorism. Our unit's operators were highly skilled in sniping, close quarters combat (CQB), explosives, dynamic and covert entry, and hand-to-hand combat. We gathered intel on terrorist threats, captured and eliminated terrorist forces and rescued hostages.

Thinking back over my 10-year military career gives me goosebumps. More so than any man ever has.

And now I'm guarding an up-and-coming supermodel.

I drop my face in my palm and sigh. *God help me.*

Don't get me wrong. I'm super grateful that Dash asked me to come work for him. He pays very well and I love our team. Eden Esposito is former CIA, Sailor Shaw and Kane Maddox are both former military, all are major badasses. It's just the lack of excitement on a daily basis that's making me edgy. I've been feeling restless lately, wondering what I can do to scratch this persistent itch for adventure.

Eden and I went shooting at the range the other day and Sailor and I went skydiving last weekend. Kane said something about going cage diving with sharks, but honestly…

Yawn.

Sitting down at my vanity, I wonder what's wrong with me. Has too much adventure early in my life left me jaded now? I pick up my new eyeshadow palette and lift the lid. A little thrill shoots through me as I check out all the gorgeous colors and I run my finger over a pretty shimmery taupe, swatching it on the back of my hand. The pigment is amazing.

Yes, my weakness is makeup and I'm not ashamed to admit it. I spend a fortune on it, collecting all sorts of lipsticks, blushes and shadows. I enjoy watching YouTube tutorials and follow my favorite makeup artists religiously. Maybe after so many years of not being able to be glamorous while in the military, I lost my mind a little. *Whatever.* I wear it every day, even if I'm just going to the grocery store, and I love it.

Of course, Maddox teases me non-stop about always being in full makeup but what does he know? The former Navy SEAL should learn to expand his horizons a little bit beyond hoarding guns and guzzling beer.

Maybe that's what I need to do, too. To be honest, I'm just not sure what's missing. There's definitely some sort of unfulfilled feeling, almost like a hole in my life, and it grows a little bigger every day. I just wish I knew how the hell to fill it.

After I finish ogling my new palette, I gather my

cosmetics and pack them just as carefully as I did my weapons. If one shadow cracks, I will be pissed.

My cosmetics case takes up more room in my small roller suitcase than my clothes and that's fine by me. All I need when it comes to my wardrobe is black. Black jeans, black t-shirt, black leather jacket and black boots.

As I zip the suitcase up, my phone beeps with a text from Eden: *on our way over with pizza and wine.*

I'm assuming Sailor is with her and they know I fly out tomorrow for New York so I'm not really in the mood to drink and have a girls' night. Guess they don't care because they're knocking on my door five minutes later.

I barely have the apartment door open before Sailor pushes through, swinging the bottle of wine and complaining about Maddox.

Here we go, I think with a resigned sigh. Those two just need to fuck and get it out of their system. But, no, they'd rather bitch to the rest of us about each other.

Eden and I exchange a shared, miserable, knowing look. The drama between Sailor and Maddox is getting to be too much to handle and off-the-charts annoying.

"Can you believe his nerve?" Sailor asks, all riled up, blonde curls bouncing indignantly.

"Sailor, can I get some wine in me before we talk about you and Maddox?" Eden begs then looks over at me, pleading with her dark brown, chestnut-colored eyes. "For the love of God, Fallon, where's the bottle opener? I'm about ready to chew this cork out with my teeth."

With a chuckle, I walk into the kitchen, grab three wine glasses, plates, napkins and an opener. Arms full, I head back and set everything on the coffee table where we all gather to eat. I don't have a table and chairs like normal people and instead always sit on my couch when I eat. Maybe it's because I'm never home enough to actually sit down and have a real meal. Or maybe it's because normally it's just me and what's the point?

As we dive into the large cheese pizza– no meat allowed since Sailor is a vegetarian– Eden fills our glasses. Even though I prefer my pizza smothered in sausage and pepperoni, when Sailor comes over I refrain from the "dead carcass toppings," as she likes to call them. "Okay, Sailor," I say. "What did Maddox do now?"

"Why doesn't anyone ever listen to me?" she demands. "I already told you how he hid my stapler and the entire time I was searching his office for it, he kept talking about *her*."

Her, of course, refers to Penelope, Maddox's girlfriend.

"Honestly, Sai, can you blame him?" Eden asks.

"*What?*" she exclaims, mouth full of pizza. "Whose side are you on?"

"The other day, you kept talking about Ben," I remind her, backing Eden up.

"So?"

"So it clearly pissed him off," I say.

"I'm not allowed to talk about how Ben surprised me with my favorite flowers?"

"Roses aren't your favorite flower," Eden says drily.

I shake my head and take a sip of wine. "Nope. Sunflowers are."

Sailor snorts but doesn't deny it and instead sucks half of her wine down. "Whatever. It was still a nice gesture and I wanted to share it with my friends at work. That's all."

Eden and I roll our eyes. "Funny that you didn't mention it all day. Then when Maddox came in-"

Sailor lifts her hand, pink painted nails flashing. "Stop right there. I know you two think something is going on between us, but the truth is we can't stand each other. I don't know what it is exactly, but we're like oil and vinegar."

"Hmm," I say, not buying it.

"It's true," she insists. "Kane Maddox is nothing but a big brute who drives me crazy 99 percent of the time."

"And what about that other one percent?" I ask with a smirk.

"That's when she's picturing that big, rock hard-"

"Eden!" Sailor gasps.

"-body of his," she finishes with an unrepentant smile. "Were you imagining some other part of him?"

"For crying out loud," Sailor exclaims, blushing to her roots. "I am not picturing...*that*."

Sailor, in all of her bubbly glory, rarely swears. It takes a helluva lot to get the girl to cuss, but I know that Maddox has coaxed a few four-letter words out of her mouth. Easily.

"Right," Eden says, not convinced. She gives her brown hair, streaked with caramel highlights, a shake. "Well, if it makes you feel any better, I can guarantee that Maddox has pictured you naked."

"That doesn't make me feel better," Sailor says in exasperation, pouring herself another glass of wine. "What about you two? I haven't heard anything lately about dates or potential love interests."

A half-laugh, half-snort bursts from Eden. "Men fucking suck. Why would I want to deal with them when I have a vibrator?"

I shake my head. It takes a lot for a man to catch my attention, but I'm not nearly as jaded as Eden when it comes to love. A bad experience a while back made her swear off men, but she's very mysterious about what happened. No one is really sure what went down and she doesn't talk about it. Eden is tough to read and that's probably what made her such an asset to the CIA.

I'm not opposed to love, but I have my doubts

that the right man for me exists. I've dated guys in the military and it inevitably resulted in a pissing contest. They challenged me to find out who can shoot better, who can reassemble their gun faster, blah, blah, blah. It got old fast and it was a no-win situation for me because if I beat them then their fragile ego bruised. If I lost then they believed I wasn't strong enough because I'm a woman and I don't have any business being beside them in combat.

Civilians are just as bad because the moment they find out about my successful military career and that I work for a private security firm, all of my badassery scares them away. Maybe the idea that I know 20 different ways to kill them in less than 10 seconds intimidates them.

I suppose I could downplay it, but why the fuck should I? I worked damn hard to make it to the top in a field that is dominated by testosterone. Besides, if they can't accept me for who I am then why should I waste my time? I'm expected to sit there and listen to them drone on about their job so I should be able to share about my day at the office, too.

Sometimes that involves shooting guns and taking down bad guys, but it's what I do.

"Fallon?" Sailor asks. "I don't even remember

the last guy who caught your eye."

"I do," Eden says with a chuckle.

I grit my teeth together and telepathically beg her not to talk about the last disaster I called a date.

But she ignores me. "How can you forget Rick?"

I cover my eyes with a hand, not wanting to relive the nightmare. "E, can we not dredge the past up?"

"Wait," Sailor says and tilts her head. "Who's Rick?"

"Someone I'd like to forget about," I grumble.

"Rick was that guy she met at the coffee shop who drove the Porsche."

Sailor bursts out laughing. "Oh, my God, I totally forgot all about him! Slickster Rickster."

I roll my eyes. *Yeah, dating civilians is the worst. They scare too easily.* "He vacated the premises so fast after seeing my weapons locker that he practically left a Rick-sized hole in my door."

"He thought she was a serial killer or something," Eden says and chuckles. "The black marks out on the street near the curb? Those are from his Porsche when he peeled away."

Eden and Sailor howl in amusement while I cross my arms with a frown. "Is it my fault that men get all insecure when I talk about my arsenal?"

"Why would you talk about that on a first date?" Sailor asks, wiping tears from her blue eyes.

"It's just who I am."

"Fallon, if a man can't handle who you are and what you've done then he isn't the right man," Eden says.

Sailor nods. "I really believe the perfect man is out there for you. But maybe next time, wait to show him your arsenal til like the third date."

I stifle a sigh as they laugh harder.

Story of my life.

Chapter Two: Ryan

"When's the last time you got laid?"

I look up from playing Call of Duty long enough to get shot in the shoulder on the big television screen in front of us. "None of your business, bro," I say.

"It was Amanda, wasn't it? I don't know whether I should laugh or cry."

I hit pause on the controller and narrow my eyes at my best friend Joe. "Since when do we discuss my sex life? Or lack of it?"

"Did you know that a man's quality of sperm starts declining at age 30 and then a more abrupt decline in male fertility starts at 45?"

For a moment, I wonder if I'm hearing him right. Never in his life has Joe Reynolds expressed any doubt about his virility and he's infamous for having a new girlfriend every other month.

"We're 32. Our swimmers are dying a little more every day, dude," he says, sounding sad.

"Are you high?" I ask, a frown creasing my brow. "Or is your paternal clock ticking, Josephina?"

"Fuck you," he grumbles. "But reading those stats got me thinking. And that's not even including those poor suckers with ED." He shudders.

"I think you need to get off Web MD," I say and grab my beer.

"FYI, alcohol kills sperm," he says, looking at my beer. "You should know that considering you almost became a doctor."

I raise a dark brow and finish swallowing. "What's up, J? You're kinda freaking me out."

"Watching my brother get married made me realize I'm nowhere even close."

"So what? You're focused on your career. I'm sure you'll meet Ms. Right at some point."

"And if I don't? Who will take care of me? Who will I leave all of my money to?"

I chuckle. "What money?"

"The fortune I plan to make."

"I think you've lost your damn mind. You're only 32 and have all the time in the world to find someone and settle down."

"Yeah, I guess you're right," he says. "I date way more than you. You're the one who should be worried. You're practically celibate with zero prospects."

I lift my middle finger and take a long sip of my beer. "For your information, it's only been…" *Fuck.* As I think back, I realize Amanda was the last woman I slept with and that was last year. "I've been busy," I remind him. "In case you forgot, I recently became a med school dropout. Time is a luxury I'm just getting used to having again."

"Is your dad handling it any better yet?"

"Dr. Allen Mercer is still extremely disappointed, but he'll live," I say, remembering the let-down look on my dad's face when I announced that I didn't want to follow in his footsteps and become a doctor.

I tried, though. I completed a four-year undergraduate program, passed the MCAT, spent four years in medical school…and hated every god-awful moment of it. I can't stand the sight of blood and guts, needles, cadavers and the medicinal smell of hospitals makes me sick.

Halfway through my residency program, I made the decision to change careers. I've always loved computers and tech stuff. I have a knack for coding and hacking. Unlike medicine, anything with a hard drive gets my blood pumping. I guess I've always been kind of a geek like that. I enjoy taking things apart, studying them and figuring out how they tick.

I spent almost ten years doing something I ended up hating and I don't regret walking away. In fact, I've never been happier. Now I'm taking some much needed me-time before I decide what the future holds.

"Oh, shit," Joe exclaims and cracks open a beer. *Apparently, he's not worried about his sperm count any longer,* I think with a wry grin. "I'm going to hook you up with Krista."

"Krista?" The name doesn't ring any bells and I remember everything.

"My Sure Thing in L.A."

"Los Angeles?" I repeat doubtfully.

"You mentioned taking a trip somewhere," he reminds me. "If you can get your ass out to Cali, I'll make sure Krista takes good care of you."

"Is she a hooker?"

"No! Just an old acquaintance," he says with a wicked grin.

"Uh-huh."

"You said it yourself– you've been working too hard. And what's better than a little fun in the SoCal sun? And a roll in the hay with Krista?"

"I don't know Krista," I remind him. "And how come you've never mentioned her?"

He stands up and moves his hands down in that wavy motion used to describe a woman with curves in all the right places. "What else do you need to know?"

"Joe-"

"You like blondes with blue eyes, right?" His eyes narrow. "Or maybe she has green eyes. I can't remember." He gives his head a shake. "Whatever, it doesn't matter. She'll get you over the Amanda slump. You'll be drought-free, my friend."

"If she's such a Sure Thing then why aren't you getting on the next flight out to L.A.?" I ask, tone wary.

"Because I think it's time I look for something more than a one-night stand. I have my deteriorating sperm to consider now."

I laugh. "You're an idiot."

"So, what do you say?" He waggles a brow and I can't believe it, but I'm actually considering it. I mean, not really the hook-up part but the vacation part. *The ocean and some sunshine sounds pretty damn good right about now,* I think as I look out the window at the gloomy, drizzle-filled New York sky.

"Get out of town, go get laid and then come back and launch your new career with a fresh mindset."

"I could use a vacation," I admit.

"I'll text Krista."

I roll my eyes. "Don't bother. I'll probably spend most of my time hanging out at the beach. Get some surfing in, rent a motorcycle and take a drive up the PCH." Hell, the more I think about it, the better it sounds. "How much do you think tickets are?"

"Probably not too bad since it's February. Lemme check." He pulls his phone out and brings up an airline with daily direct flights from NYC to LA. "Only three hundred bucks if you can leave the day after tomorrow."

"My schedule is pretty clear. I mean, the no job thing kinda helps."

Joe starts typing my information into the reservations section. "Got a frequent flyer number?"

I rattle off the 20-digit code, a mix of letters and numerals.

"It's so weird to me that you can do that," he mumbles, typing away.

I shrug. "Comes in handy."

"You're the only person I know who has a photographic memory. You do realize that's why we became best friends, right? Because in high school, I would sit by you so I could cheat off you."

"You're such a dickhead."

"Just kidding. Kind of."

After another minute of filling out the form online, he asks for my credit card and I tell him the numbers, expiration date and security code on the back without even thinking. Having a photographic memory has been both a blessing and a curse. In school, I absorbed everything like a sponge. It's why I never got anything less than an A from first grade through med school.

Sometimes it's weird to be able to close my eyes and see an object or information in my mind's eye in great detail. It's like I can take a mental snapshot and then recall the image without error. Without even concentrating, I can visualize people I've seen for only a few minutes down to the most minute detail including hairstyle, clothing, jewelry, tattoos and makeup.

It's not so great when I just want to clear my brain of useless crap and forget things, though.

"Boom! You're on the 10am flight Thursday morning to LaLa Land. Don't forget to pack condoms," Joe says, mouth edging up.

"You're insane, you know that?"

"Maybe a little," he admits.

I shake my head, turn my attention back to the image frozen on the TV screen and hit play. More shooting and my poor guy goes down in a bloody death.

Well, I never claimed to be a warrior. I hit reset and start over.

Chapter Three: Fallon

When Thursday morning arrives, I've been in New York City less than 24 hours and have gone over the plan and itinerary with Sierra Simone, my client, several times. I take everything into account while on a mission and have a backup plan for my backup plan.

We made our way through security at JFK without incident. I checked my container of weapons and other goodies, the case locked up tight, and will see it when we land at LAX.

"Let's grab a latte," Sierra says and heads toward Starbucks.

Of course, the line is around the corner and I'm

still trying to figure out when everyone became so jazzed about spending seven bucks on a coffee. I suppose caffeine is an addiction, though, and people will pay anything to get their high.

It takes almost 25 minutes to reach the register and I glance down at my watch impatiently.

"What do you want, Fallon? My treat."

"I'm fine," I say. "But thank you."

"You don't like coffee?" she asks, blue eyes widening.

Not seven-dollar, over-hyped chain coffees that taste like crap, I think. "I'm a bit of a coffee snob," I admit.

"Ahh," she says. "So, you like the good stuff. You pick out your beans and grind them yourself?"

I nod.

"I love that! We did that when I was on a shoot in Guatemala," she gushes and then turns to the cashier. "I'll have a venti nonfat, iced skinny mocha with light ice, whipped cream and no chocolate drizzle."

While she pays an absurd amount of money for her caffeine-laced, venti-sized cup of diabetes-light, I scan the area and make sure no one looks suspicious. I've yet to spot Sierra's stalker, but I don't doubt her or take the job lightly. Every mission I go on, I go all in and give it my utmost attention. Even though I'm craving excitement, I know Sierra would be much happier if the man harassing her stays in New York City while she jets off to Los Angeles.

After getting her coffee, which takes another ten minutes, we walk to the gate and I motion for her to follow me over to a couple of seats that face the entire area. I have a great view of the airport traffic coming and going plus a clear visual of the passengers in the convenience store across the way. Alert, yet not expecting any issues, I lean back in my chair and cross a booted foot on my opposite knee.

"Oh, I love your boots," Sierra exclaims.

"Thanks."

Sierra turns in her seat and leans forward, coffee clasped in her hands. "So how in the world does someone as gorgeous as you start working for a private security company? Because when you showed up at my door, I'm not going to lie– I was a little surprised."

"Were you expecting some ex-military hunk?" I ask, mouth edging up.

She nods. "More like hoping. Realistically, I figured I'd probably get guarded by some aging P.I. with a bald spot."

I chuckle. "First of all, thank you. And you're the one who's gorgeous, by the way."

She waves my compliment away with a flick of her wrist. Sierra Simone is tall, blonde and beautiful. Super slim like most runway models and I can only imagine how much designers and their clothes must love her. "I have a feeling that you lead an exciting life and I want to hear all about it."

With a little shrug, I think about how bored I've been lately. "I am ex-military," I tell her and her blue eyes widen. "I spent 10 years taking down the bad guys and after separating from the Army, my former commander hired me to work at his company."

"Dash, right? That low, velvety voice of his made me want to lick my phone."

I've never heard anyone describe Dash Slater's voice as velvety and I bite back a laugh. I can admit he's a good-looking guy, but he's like my brother. "I don't know about that, but Dash is the owner and the one you spoke with when you called."

"That man must be hot as all get-out because he

had my kitty purring just from the tone of his voice. Is he single?"

Oh, Lord. I pinch the bridge of my nose. Sierra is sweet but I am not going to discuss how she's lusting after my boss. "He's a workaholic," I say and let my gaze move over the passengers gathering at the gate. The plane takes off in less than an hour and they should start letting us board soon. Hopefully really soon so any further inappropriate conversation about Dash Slater can come to an end. "Wait a second. Didn't you mention having a boyfriend?"

Sierra gives me a coy smile. "Armand," she says with a little sigh. "It's not exactly official yet because we haven't announced anything, but he's sweet to me. The man has more money than…well, anybody." She lowers her voice and says, "He's a prince."

"Really?"

"Yep. I can't remember the name of the country, but it's somewhere in Europe. Oh, and my birthday is coming up and he gave me a card with hints about my present. I don't really understand all his little clues, but I'm hoping it's jewelry. What about you?" she asks and takes a sip of coffee.

"What about me?" I ask carefully. *God, she's*

chatty.

"Are you married? Dating anyone? Single with your eye on someone perhaps?" She lifts her perfectly-manicured brows in a waggle.

"Happily single," I say, voice flat. I'm ready to end this conversation before it even begins.

"Ooh, sounds to me like you got burned. Do tell."

Luckily, an airline employee interrupts us with an announcement about boarding. Our seats are in Business Class so we'll be getting on soon. "Why don't we go up there and wait?" I suggest and grab the handle of my small roller suitcase.

With a nod, Sierra pops up and we head over to wait with a small gathering of passengers. I scan over the people standing with us and immediately feel a set of eyes on me. I glance over and see a man with brown hair, short on the sides but longer and kind of messy on the top. He's cleanly-shaven and has dark brown eyes.

The moment I meet his gaze, he looks away and shifts awkwardly. He's wearing a pair of worn jeans and a t-shirt that says "There are 10 types of people in this world. Those who understand binary and those who don't."

I have no idea what that means, but I'm guessing it's some kind of nerd humor. *He's harmless.* I turn back to Sierra who's scrolling through her phone, madly searching for her boarding pass, no doubt. I reach down and pull mine out of the side pocket of my suitcase.

A few minutes later, they invite our section to board and I motion for Sierra to go first. She finally finds her digital boarding pass and runs it over the scanner. I hand mine to the airline attendant, she swipes it over the reader and hands it back to me. "Have a good flight," she says.

With a nod, I follow Sierra onto the jetway and we slowly make our way down and board the plane. I hate flying commercial. It sucks in every possible way from long lines to crowds to security to now sitting in this big tin can with a bunch of strangers and hoping no one turns out to be a raving lunatic with a death wish. Unfortunately, Eden needed the company's private jet for another job, so I got stuck dealing with this.

"Mind if I sit by the window?" Sierra asks and plops down next to it without waiting for my answer. She starts blowing up a ring to put around her neck and already has a silk mask up on her forehead.

Oh, thank God, I think, and mentally sigh in relief. She plans to sleep the next six hours so I don't have to dodge her prying questions. "Go right ahead," I say, looking forward to blessed silence. I heave my suitcase up, slide it into the overhead bin and sit down.

A moment later, the aisle starts getting crowded and someone bumps into my shoulder.

"Sorry," a deep voice says.

Now that is a velvety voice, I think.

I look up and see the guy with the geeky saying on his shirt. Forcing a smile, I turn my attention to the screen on the seat in front of me, deciding whether I should put a movie on or listen to my music. He bangs into me again and my whole chair rattles. Gritting my teeth, I wish more than anything we were on Slater Security's private plane with Eric Finn, pilot extraordinaire, at the controls.

Glancing up, I watch Binary Guy struggling to shove his carry-on in the bin above me and he's so close that he's practically brushing against me. Normally I'd feel uncomfortable but for some odd reason I don't. He smells good, too. Clean like Ivory soap and laundry detergent.

His bag must've gotten stuck on someone else's

luggage or simply doesn't fit, but he's determined. He gives it a hard yank and I get the feeling it's going to fall on my head. A second later, he pulls harder and it pops out and drops.

I lift my hands to cover my head but luckily he manages to grab it at the last second.

"I am so sorry!" His face flushes.

"It's fine," I say, noticing that he has really nice eyes, a deep brown that reminds me of good espresso. "I don't think it's going to fit there, though."

"I think you're right," he agrees and turns around to put it in the overhead bin across the narrow aisle.

My gaze lands on the back of his broad shoulders and dips down to a mighty-fine ass encased in denim. I look away and give myself a mental shake. I don't normally ogle strange men like this and it occurs to me that maybe it's been a little too long since I've had sex. *Hmm.* Maybe I should just get a vibrator like Eden.

After he sits down in front of us, I lean back into my seat and glance over at Sierra. The plane hasn't even moved yet and she's already out like a light. *Must be nice.*

Me, on the other hand, I have to stay vigilant.

Three hours later, I eat a granola bar, drink a bottle of water and pretend to watch a movie. But really, I'm watching Binary Guy between the seats. He puts on a pair of glasses and opens a laptop. Angling myself just right, I can see him working on...

Hell, I have no idea what he's doing. Lots of zeros and ones fill the screen and I think he must be coding or doing some kind of tech stuff. I watch his fingers move over the keyboard and something about it soothes me. He has really nice hands, too. Big and competent-looking with long fingers.

I let out a little sigh. It's been so long since I've had a man's hands on me. Turning away, I check on Sierra who is so sound asleep that she's lightly snoring. Short of the plane crashing, I don't think anything is going to wake her up.

Unbuckling my seatbelt, I decide to make a quick trip to the bathroom. I drank too much water and there's no way my bladder is going to hold for another few hours. Standing up, I walk over to the lavatory and, of course, three people stand in front of me, already waiting.

It's funny how no one ever has to pee until we're all crammed on an airplane. As the thought flutters through my head, I glance up and see Binary Guy heading over. He stops right beside me and looks over the crowd gathering.

"It's funny how no one has to go until we're all on a plane together," he says, practically echoing my thought.

I look up into his dark brown eyes and all I can think of is chocolate mousse. He's still wearing the black-rimmed glasses. I've never found a man in eyeglasses sexy before, but, holy hell, this guy really knows how to pull it off. A strange shyness comes over me and my gaze dips to his shirt. It's starting to bother me that I don't understand the saying on it. I'll have to google it when I get back to my seat.

Suddenly, the plane hits a patch of turbulence and we all bounce. I grab the nearest seat to steady myself with one hand and see Binary Guy stumble forward. Without even thinking, I automatically reach out and grab his arm. *Hello, muscles.* The thick, hard cords in his upper arm catch me by surprise. Guess Binary Guy works out.

He regains his balance, stands up straight and, like an idiot, I'm still holding his arm. Our gazes lock and I swear he flexes his arm, which makes me snap back to attention. I let go and run a hand through my loose, dark hair.

"Thanks," he says.

He's taller than I thought, maybe 6'2" or so, and considering I'm almost 5'8", I've always gravitated toward tall men. "Sorry," I mumble, gaze once again focusing on the words written across his chest.

"You speak binary?" he asks, mouth edging up.

My gaze snaps up to look into his dark eyes. "What?"

He points to his shirt.

Suddenly, I feel like an uneducated moron. "Um, no."

"It means there are only *two* types of people in the world: those who understand binary and those who don't."

I frown. It still doesn't make any damn sense to me. I've never been very savvy when it comes to math or science. I excel at hunting enemies down and shooting guns. *You know. Practical shit.*

"See, this looks like the number ten," he says and points to the "10."

"Uh-huh."

"But, actually, it's two."

"Two?" I repeat blankly.

"The binary system is made up of 1's and 0's. So, 10 is two, not the number ten. If you understand then you know the quote actually says there are only two types of people-" He abruptly stops. "I'll shut up now."

A small smile curves my mouth. Damn, he's adorable in a dorky kind of way. But *so* not my type. I've never dated anyone like him and, if I had to guess, we are probably opposites in every way. Not that it matters. Relationships just don't work for me.

Suddenly the bathroom door opens and it's finally my turn. "Thanks for the lesson," I say and head inside the tiny, crammed area. After securely locking the door, I lean against the sink and swipe a stray wisp of hair back.

What the fuck was that?

And why is my heart beating so fast?

******

The moment we land at Los Angeles International Airport, Sierra wakes up. She slept the entire flight and I'm a little envious of anyone who has the talent to sleep through a whole plane ride from one coast to the other.

We head down to the crowded baggage claim and I can't help but look for Binary Guy. Even though he gave off total geek vibes, he also had something very physically appealing going on. My black carry case of weapons arrives and I pull it off the luggage carousel, setting it down beside my small roller suitcase. Sierra has six suitcases and I have a feeling we're going to be here forever waiting for all of her crap.

The man next to us pushes his way through to get to the rotating conveyor belt and stands there, blocking us now, and his bags are nowhere in sight. *Why do people do that?* I wonder. So annoying.

While Sierra searches for her bags, another couple of people sneak through and I cross my arms, aggravated.

"People are so rude," a deep voice says near my ear.

I glance over and there he is, looking a little rumpled, glasses hanging from the neck of his t-shirt.

"They really are," I agree.

From the corner of my eye, I see Sierra

struggling to grab her passing suitcase. Before I can step in and help, Binary Guy grabs it, easily swinging it up and off the belt, even though I know it weighs well over 50 pounds because she had to pay extra.

"Thank you," she says and bats her lashes. "Aren't you the gentleman?"

Sierra is such a flirt and the way she's looking at him bothers me way more than it should. She isn't even trying to hide the fact that she's checking him out. It's beyond transparent and I let out an annoyed sigh.

"No problem," he says.

"I'm Sierra." She extends a hand.

"Ryan," he says, and I feel all sorts of prickly annoyance when they touch.

"And that's Fallon," she says. When he glances at me, I force a smile then look away and someone else bumps into me. *God, I hate flying commercial,* I think for the thousandth time.

"So, Ryan, what're you doing in L.A.?" Sierra asks.

"Just a vacation."

"Oh, look, that's mine, too. Would you mind grabbing it?" She nods at a big suitcase on its way down.

"Yeah, sure," he says.

My gaze inevitably moves back over to Ryan's posterior as he leans over and easily heaves her 80-pound suitcase off the belt. She has two luggage carts and he stacks her stuff on them neatly.

Ryan. Nice name, nice guy, nice ass. So not for me. I don't do nice in any capacity.

While they chat it up and wait for the rest of her bags, I cross my arms with a scowl and look through the large glass window facing the curb. Our driver should be waiting to take us to the hotel. I pull my phone out and double check the information the car company texted me earlier. It should be a black Suburban and the driver's name is Manuel.

Twenty torturous minutes later, I am ready to jet. This is why I never check luggage. It takes an eternity. Poor Ryan has had his small black suitcase forever, but he stays and keeps helping Sierra. *Of course, he does.* She's a gorgeous model and he clearly likes being at her beck and call.

When the last piece is finally loaded, I grab one

of the carts and throw my two suitcases on top. "Let's go," I huff, pushing it toward the exit.

Sierra gives Ryan a little shrug, a quick thank you and tugs the second cart with a grunt.

"Need any help?" he asks her.

I stifle a groan. As if he hasn't helped enough. Hell, why doesn't he just follow us back to our hotel and unpack all her stuff, too? Make sure it's all ironed and hung up while he's at it?

Ryan places his case on top and pushes, following me outside to the curb. I find the Suburban and wave to the driver who gets out and opens the back. Both men are practically tripping over each other as they load up all the luggage.

"You're just so strong," Sierra gushes.

I'm done. "Are you ready?" I ask between gritted teeth, ushering Sierra toward the rear passenger side door. She gets in and when she lifts her hand to wave goodbye, I motion for her to slide over.

"Scooch," I say. Once inside, I promptly shut the door and cross my arms. The driver maneuvers the SUV forward, inching us toward the airport exit.

"Wasn't he sweet?" she asks.

"Sweet as sugar," I say, voice dripping with sarcasm. "I'm sure Armand would love him," I add a little meanly. But Sierra doesn't seem to notice and continues to ramble on so I tune her out.

Since I live right down in San Diego, I've been to L.A. quite a number of times. So, when our driver heads onto the 405 S, the opposite direction of Beverly Hills, I frown. Of course, Sierra appears clueless. "Excuse me? You're going the wrong way."

When he ignores me, a warning light flashes in my brain. My case full of weapons is in the back and I turn around, looking for it. An uneasy feeling trickles through my gut and the need to have my Glock in hand overwhelms me.

The driver accelerates, weaving through traffic, and I shove luggage aside, searching for my black case. *Where the hell is it?*

It takes a minute, but Sierra finally catches on. "Um, sir? I think Beverly Hills is that way," she says and points behind us.

"We're not going to Beverly Hills. Turn around and sit down," he growls, glaring at me through the rear view mirror.

Shitshitshit. I finally spot my case and yank it up and over the seat. I reach down for the key, tucked away in my boot, pluck it out and shove it into the keyhole. But when I turn, nothing happens. I jiggle it and try again. Nothing. *Dammit.*

I slide my thumbs over the latches and blink in surprise when the lid pops open. Lifting it up, I see jeans, t-shirts and a toiletry bag. Confused, my gaze lands on the tag hanging from the handle and my stomach sinks. I flip it over and read "Ryan Mercer" followed by a New York address and phone number. *Son of a fucking bitch.*

Our luggage got mixed up and now all of my weapons are gone.

Chapter Four: Ryan

Los Angeles traffic is ungodly awful but luckily I make pretty decent timing to my hotel over in Santa Monica. It helps that I'm staying on the West side and not too far from the airport. After I get out of the Uber, I pause to look out over the ocean.

It's been a while since I've seen the Pacific and she is a damn welcoming sight for sore eyes. Joe was right. I needed this trip more than I realized.

After checking in, I head up to my room, drop my small suitcase and carry-on down on the bed and throw open the balcony doors. Breathing in deeply, I savor the salty ocean air and the sound of seagulls squawking. The sun is high overhead and there's a small crowd of people lying down on the beach. I plan to do all sorts of relaxing down there, too.

A handful of surfers ride the medium-sized waves and even though I haven't been surfing in a while, I'm looking forward to getting out there and scraping the rust off. Leaning forward, I rest my arms on the balcony railing and think about the gorgeous, dark-haired woman from the flight.

Talk about stunning. She was some Catherine Zeta Jones/ Angelina Jolie hybrid that I can't believe I actually talked to. I get nervous speaking to women I find attractive, but Fallon was on an entirely different level than any other woman I have ever met.

With long, dark hair and amazing blue-green eyes the shade of the sea, I think she knocked the breath out of me when I first laid eyes on her. And what did I do? I talked to her about binary numbers. *God, I'm an idiot.*

I've never had a lot of game or finesse when it came to impressing women with witty repartee, but I do alright if she has a soft spot for geeky, nice guys who have manners. Intelligent banter sometimes works for me, but with Zeta/Jolie? I don't think I've ever been so tongue-tied. The word smitten crosses my mind and I sigh.

I know nothing ever– and I mean *ever*– would've happened between us, but I can dream. I'm never going to see her again, but I'll always have the memory of the woman who made my breath catch. Guess it was nice while it lasted.

Turning around, I walk back into the room to unpack. I reach down and attempt to pop the latches on my suitcase but nothing happens. Frowning, I lean over and push harder, assuming they're jammed, but the damn thing won't open.

"What the hell?" I mumble. I never lock it so that's not the problem. TSA probably checked through it and then locked it by accident, thinking I had locked it originally. They have keys to open anything and this actually happened to me once before.

Luckily, suitcase locks are flimsy and all I need is a paperclip to pop the sucker open. Turning to the nightstand, I pull the drawer out and search. *Nope.* Just a Bible and some travel brochures. My gaze moves over the room and I walk to the desk, pull the drawer open and *bazinga!*

Paperclip.

I grab it, straightening it as I walk back to the bed, sit down, and drag the suitcase over. I shove the metal end into the keyhole and twist it around. I saw a video on lockpicking once and thought it would be a fun skill to learn. Never actually thought I'd need it, though. Almost five full minutes later, it's still not budging. The damn thing feels cemented shut.

Huh. My gaze drops down to the luggage tag and I do a double take because mine isn't leather like this. *Oh, shit.* I lift the flap up and instead of my name, I see "Fallon Pierce" and a San Diego address and phone number.

Holy shit. I accidentally grabbed Fallon's luggage.

Fallon. As in Zeta/Jones, hottest woman on the planet, who probably thinks I'm the biggest geek since Sheldon Cooper. I obviously mixed our luggage up when I was helping her friend and loading everything into the back of the SUV. The small, black roller suitcases are identical so it was an easy mistake to make.

This is why people tie little, brightly-colored ribbons on their plain black suitcases.

I suppose the good news is now I get to call her and set up a meeting so we can swap luggage. The idea of seeing her again makes my heart trip in my chest. I know she's probably going to be annoyed, though. Even though she was gorgeous, she didn't seem to possess a lot of patience.

I'm damn curious, too, about why the locks on her suitcase are reinforced. *What the hell does she have in here?* I wonder and tap a finger against the lid.

Not having an answer to a question bothers me. My brain is wired in such a way that it demands to know things. Right now, I want to know why her suitcase is sealed up tighter than Fort Knox.

As I'm debating whether or not to call her, my phone rings. I check the screen and see "unknown caller." Taking a deep breath, I slide the bar over. "Hello?"

"Ryan?"

"Yes," I answer, instantly recognizing that breathy voice that belongs to Fallon.

"I have your suitcase. They must've gotten mixed up."

"Yeah," I say, looking down at hers. "Definitely seems to have been a mix-up."

Her silence fills the line for a moment too long.

Then, she asks, "Did you open it?"

"Are you kidding? No one's getting in this sucker without the key."

It sounds like she breathes a sigh of relief.

"So, what're you hiding?" I ask.

"I'm sorry, what?"

"Do you have weapons or drugs in here? Special CIA gadgets?" It's clear that she's traveling with items that she doesn't want anyone else to have access to, which makes me think she's a cop. Maybe a secret agent. Or what if she's a highly-paid assassin? My mind is going wild with possible scenarios.

"It's none of your business," she states tartly. When I don't respond, her voice drops. "You opened it, didn't you?"

I really don't like being accused of something I didn't do, and it sparks an urge to play with her. Maybe because she's wound a little too tight. And, well, it's kind of fun.

"If I say yes, are you going to kill me?" I'm joking, of course, and I'm curious how she's going to respond.

A heavy sigh fills my ear. "I'd appreciate it if you didn't go through my personal things," she says in a taut voice.

"And I'd appreciate it if you didn't look through mine, either," I say, unable to resist teasing her.

"I didn't," she huffs in an indignant voice.

"Then how did you know you had my suitcase?"

"I-" She makes an annoyed sound. "Listen, Ryan Mercer. I want my gear back now. So let's set up a place to meet and swap suitcases."

Gear? A smile curves my mouth. Damn, she's feisty. All business, no play, and it's kind of fun riling her up. "Okay. Where?"

"Where are you?"

"Oh, wouldn't you like to know, Mrs. Smith?"

"What?" Confusion laces her voice.

"Did you ever see Mr. & Mrs. Smith? With Angelina Jolie and Brad Pi-"

"What does that have to do with anything?" she snaps.

"She was a spy and, well, you look a lot like her," I say.

Silence again. Then she clears her throat. "Meet me on the Santa Monica Pier. Can you be there in an hour?"

The Santa Monica Pier is five minutes away, and the boardwalk that extends over the ocean full of restaurants, touristy shops and amusement park-style rides is already on my list of things I want to do. There's also a cart there with the best churros ever.

"Sure," I say. "Why don't we meet by the roller coaster?"

"See you in 59 minutes. And don't be late," she says and hangs up.

I stare at my phone for a minute too long and can't help but grin. Fallon Pierce is a grumpy force to be reckoned with and she has me all kinds of interested. The last woman I dated, Amanda, was a quiet, people-pleaser who I met during my residency last year. Having a conversation with her was like pulling teeth sometimes and she had this perma-grin that seemed sweet at first but then just started to creep me out.

Amanda and I dated for a few months, but our

lives were far too busy for anything serious. Honestly, I think we both needed an outlet, a way to release tension after a stressful day at the hospital. Mostly, we just had quickies in the supply closet. At the time, it's all I wanted, all either of us needed.

But Fallon Pierce is a completely different type of woman. If Amanda is a kitten then Fallon is a panther. Tall, sleek and dressed all in black. When my lonely dick begins to respond, I grit my teeth. *Ain't gonna happen, pal. Don't even start getting excited. She's way out of your league.*

I have nearly 45 minutes until I get to see my dream girl again and I'm thinking it might go better if I freshen up. I still have the lovely scent of airplane on me and, even though I can't change my clothes since she has them all, I can still take a quick shower before I walk over to the pier.

With images of ebony hair and tempting blue-green eyes in my head, I end up taking a really cold shower.

Chapter Five: Fallon

After hanging up with Binary Guy– I mean Ryan– my head begins to throb and I massage my temples. *So far, we're off to a terrific start,* I think dryly. Nearly abducted by our driver and all of my weapons are gone.

At least I still have my makeup, I think. Losing my new palette and all my beauty supplies would've really made me blow a fuse.

When Sierra and I were in that SUV with the man who clearly wasn't Manuel, I knew I had to get her to safety fast. My heart sank when I saw the luggage tag that said "Ryan Mercer" while we were speeding along the 405 S, as fast as traffic would allow, anyway, in the opposite direction of The Beverly Hills Hotel where we were supposed to have been driven.

Luckily, L.A. traffic is predictable in the fact that it always and inevitably comes to a standstill. I had no plans to jump out of a moving vehicle with Sierra. But stopping did give me the opportunity to surprise the driver without killing us in a collision.

I exchange a look with Sierra that I hope calms her and reassures her that I have a solution to our current dilemma. Even though I'm still working it out in my head. The driver glances back at us every so often in the rear view mirror but I don't think he's too concerned. We're just two defenseless women, right?

Ha.

I reach down, flip the heel of my boot open and wrap my fingers around the small pocket knife hidden inside. Clicking the heel shut, I slide up and, in one swift move, I flick the knife open and press the sharp edge of the blade into the driver's thick neck.

Not expecting the move, he hits the gas, swerves the wheel and we careen into the left lane, nearly hitting another car. Horns blare and I press down hard until the knife pierces his skin and a crimson drop of blood appears.

"Pull over," I hiss in his ear. "Do it now or I'll slit your throat." The tone of my voice convinces him that I'm not playing.

"Fuck!" he swears and starts making his way across five lanes of traffic.

Sliding a hand down, I pat for a gun at his waist, but don't feel anything. Of course that doesn't mean there's not one stashed in the glove box or beneath his seat. "Hands up in the 10 and 2 position," I snap the moment his hands slip lower. I push the blade deeper for emphasis and he grunts.

After cutting off a slew of angry Angelenos, we pull off the freeway and he slams on the brakes.

"Now you're going to get out," I tell him. "Slowly."

His left hand drops down to open the door. "You're gonna regret this," he says, jerking the handle up.

"Doubtful," I respond. "Now get the hell out before I sink this blade into your carotid artery and watch you bleed out."

He carefully slides out of the vehicle and I quickly realize that I'm at a considerable disadvantage hanging over the front seat. Luckily, he seems too distraught at the blood dripping down his neck to notice.

"Shut the door," I say, and he slams it without argument. I hop up into the front seat as fast as possible and press down on the locks.

"Holy shit!" Sierra cries from behind me. She launches herself against the seat and looks over at me, blue eyes wide as saucers. "Who was that guy?"

"No idea," I say and put the SUV into drive. Hitting the gas, I drive along the side of the road before I can slip back into traffic.

Now, at our hotel in Beverly Hills, I think over everything that happened and something isn't right. I hate being caught off-guard and the fact that all of my weapons are with Ryan Mercer makes me very uneasy.

Before I meet him, though, I need to speak with Sierra because I have a niggling feeling that she isn't being completely honest with me. My gut is telling me there's more to the story than she's letting on. Today's abduction was carefully orchestrated.

Sierra and I are sharing a large suite and the

moment I hear the shower stop, I head over to her side of the room. Steam pours out when she steps from the bathroom wearing a fluffy white hotel robe, hair wrapped up in a towel.

"We need to talk," I say.

"About what?"

Even now I can hear the uneasy lilt in her voice that makes me think she isn't being completely truthful with me. Sierra Simone may be a world-class model, but she can't act her way out of a paper bag.

"You said you needed personal protection because you have a stalker," I say.

"That's right. Well, technically, I have a few."

"What aren't you telling me, Sierra? I can't fully protect you if you're keeping secrets from me."

Her pretty face falls and she cracks. "I know. I'm sorry, Fallon. You're right."

I wait as she wrings her hands.

"I sort of have something in my possession that some bad people might want."

"What?" I ask, my hackles instantly rising.

"Remember how I told you my birthday is coming up and Armand gave me a card with hints about my present?"

"Yes."

"Well, I called him right before my shower and told him what happened. He said they must've found out."

"Who found out what?" I ask darkly.

"That he was gifting me Cupid's Bow."

I frown, trying to figure out why that sounds so familiar. Sierra walks over to her purse, pulls a card out and hands it to me.

"That's what they wanted," she says.

I flip it open and skim over all the lovey-dovey crap in small, slanted handwriting. At the end, right before his signature, there's a long string of code made up of letters, numbers and symbols. "What is this?" I ask.

"It's the combination to a safe that holds my birthday present– Cupid's Bow."

The name clicks. "The priceless ruby necklace?"

"Uh-huh. It's a ruby in the shape of a heart. Armand just told me it's like $5 million. It's kind of famous."

"Cupid's Bow," I repeat, unable to believe it. *Kind of famous?* Oh, Lord, I am so close to smacking my palm against my forehead. Either that or throttling Sierra. The Cupid's Bow ruby necklace is a privately-owned piece of jewelry that celebrities have worn down red carpets with an army of security detail trailing behind them. I know because I was part of an entourage when it graced Sandra Bullock's neck one year at the Academy Awards. "I've heard of it. So where exactly is it?"

"In a safe out here, at his Bel Air house. Armand is planning to fly in for the fashion show and then we're going to open it together. But, in case he gets stuck in Andorra, he wanted me to have the combination so I can open it on my birthday."

"This changes everything," I say, eyes on the card. "Whoever you thought was your stalker is probably a jewel thief and has been trailing you." No doubt about it. I'd be willing to bet my last dollar that someone wants that necklace. Now it's up to me to protect Sierra and her jewelry. "I'm going to call Dash and see what he thinks. In the meantime, I need to meet Ryan and get my case back."

"I can't believe your luggage got mixed up. Kind of fate, though."

"What do you mean?" I ask, trying to play it cool, as I pull my leather jacket on.

"He's a-freaking-dorable! Don't tell me you didn't notice."

Is he? I wouldn't use the word adorable. More like interesting maybe. Or dorky, I try to convince myself. *Oh, who the hell am I kidding?* He was totally adorable and had an ass that begged to be squeezed. I clench my hands into fists, nails digging into my palms.

"He's fine," I say, keeping my expression and voice neutral. "Not my usual type. Anyway, all I care about is getting my gear back. Especially now that I know you have the code to a safe holding a $5 million necklace, and unknown tangoes after you."

"What's a tango?" she asks.

"That's military-speak for an enemy."

"Ooh, this is getting exciting, huh?"

I sigh. This is *so not* what I'd planned for. Thank

goodness I brought more weapons than I originally thought I'd need. Who knows who I'm up against? I suppose the good thing is I'm only a couple of hours away from Slater Security. If I need backup, they can be here in a heartbeat.

"Can I hold onto this?" I ask and lift the card. When she nods, I tuck it into the inside pocket of my jacket.

Fortunately, The Beverly Hills Hotel is a fortress with its own private security detail and a safe place for celebrities to frolic. I'm not overly concerned about leaving Sierra for an hour or two. Even so, I'm going to make sure one of their undercover security officers stays on her like glue. For an exorbitant tip, it shouldn't be a problem. I glance down at my watch. "Stay in the room and lock the door behind me. I'll be back soon."

"Tell Ryan I said hi," she says with a wink.

Rolling my eyes, I walk out. We ditched the SUV a couple of miles away in case it had a GPS locator on it so I grab an Uber and head to Santa Monica. On the ride over, I think about the exquisite ruby necklace and that Sierra is dating the prince of Andorra. *Unbelievable.* This definitely changes the game but I'm always down for a challenge. I'll call Dash after getting my gear back and catch him up. Just in case things go south and I need that backup.

Ryan Mercer. Thoughts of his dark brown eyes make me shift in my seat. It's obvious that he's incredibly intelligent and I've never dated a really smart man like that before. In the cerebral sense, I mean. The men I've dated have mostly been former military and some of them possessed bigger arms than brains.

Not that there's anything wrong with military men. I fucking love them and I practically am one of them– if not for my ovaries and uterus, anyway.

As we pull up to the Santa Monica Pier, I give my hair a fluff and can't explain the sudden flutter in my belly. I take a deep breath, shove the car door open and pull Ryan's suitcase out.

Just get your gear and call it a day. No biggie.

And there's certainly no reason to look into those deep, dark brown eyes of his for longer than a moment.

Chapter Six: Ryan

While waiting for Fallon to arrive, I play with the small piece of rope that I always carry around, tying and untying knots. Some people squeeze stress balls, I prefer working knots.

The moment I see the badass extraordinaire herself, I stuff the rope back into my pocket. It's like the crowd parts to allow Fallon Pierce room to walk. She has this incredible presence about her that makes me stand up and take notice. Pushing off the edge of the railing where my hip is perched, I lift a hand and start walking over to meet her, pulling her suitcase along over the uneven, wooden boardwalk.

"Sorry about the mixup," I say and smile. Damn,

she's gorgeous. Still dressed all in black and looking ready to beat somebody up.

She reaches for the handle of her luggage and pulls it close as the roller coaster roars by behind us. "I'm just glad to have it back," she says. "I hope you aren't lying about not opening it."

What the hell is she hiding? I wonder for the hundredth time. I think it's kind of fun letting her believe that I looked through her stuff, though. Keeps her guessing. "Well, we both know that you opened mine. Somehow, I don't think my stuff is quite as interesting as yours," I tease and her seafoam eyes narrow.

"No," she finally says. "Your boxer shorts with trains on them aren't that interesting."

A flush creeps up my neck. "Did you see the pair with palm trees? I thought they'd be good for the trip."

When a smile cracks, it feels good knowing I made it happen. Damn, she gives off uptight and serious vibes. She really needs to loosen up and relax, but I have a feeling that any man who suggests such a thing would get a boot to the throat.

"Where are you staying?" I ask. "Sierra mentioned being here for a fashion show."

"We're in Beverly Hills."

"Aww, man, coming all the way over here was a trek."

"It wasn't that bad."

"When is L.A. traffic not bad?" I ask and cock my head.

"I would've flown to the moon to get my case back," she admits.

Yep, she's got important, mysterious stuff in there. "C'mon" I say and motion for her to follow me. "They sell the best churro you will ever taste at that cart right there. My treat."

"Um." She hesitates.

"Would I steer you wrong?"

"I don't know," she says and props a hand on her hip. "I don't know you."

"When it comes to dessert and computers, you can trust me." I lift my chin and beckon her over. "I won't bite, Fallon."

I turn around and head toward the cart, leaving her standing there. If I had to guess, a woman like

Fallon can't resist a challenge. When I hear her follow me, I suppress a grin.

"What the hell is a churro, anyway?" she grumbles, eyeing the cart suspiciously.

"A sugar and cinnamon delight," I say and order two from the man. "Can you add some extra on there?"

Fallon watches him dust the fried dough sticks in an additional coating of sweetness and my mouth waters. But it's got nothing to do with the churro and everything to do with the gorgeous woman beside me.

After paying, I hand one over to her. "How can you live in Southern California and not know what a churro is?"

She shrugs and takes it. "Oh, it's warm."

With a nod, I bite into mine and watch as she does the same. Her eyes slide shut in delight and her tongue flicks out to lick away some excess sugar and cinnamon from her lips. Suppressing a groan, I swallow. For some reason, I get the feeling that she has no idea how sexy she is. God, this woman intrigues me.

"How long are you in town?" I ask, wanting to get a conversation going with her. One that's more than just a couple of words on her end. Suddenly I want to know everything about her. I know I'm not the biggest or strongest or best-looking guy in the room, but I can ooze charm and impress with my humor when I want to.

"Just a couple of days. I'm escorting Sierra back to New York after the fashion show."

"Escorting?" She merely nods. "You're very secretive," I say and take another bite of my churro as we walk down the boardwalk.

"I don't normally spill my guts to strangers."

I abruptly stop walking and turn to face her. "I'm Ryan Mercer, 32 years old, from Buffalo. I dropped out of med school recently because after way too many years, I finally concluded it wasn't for me and my happiness was more important than my dad's. He's a doctor, by the way," I add. "As you may assume, he was disappointed, but I am finally free to do what I love. And that will most likely revolve around me starting my own IT company. Or I'll just work as a hacker on the Dark Web doing questionable jobs for secret organizations like the one you probably work for."

I hold my hand out. Surprise and amusement

flash through her blue-green eyes. They glitter like aquamarines in the sunlight and I hope she doesn't tell me to go screw. To my relief, she takes my hand in hers and shakes it. Her grip is firm and I can feel calluses.

"And what would give you that idea, Mr. Mercer?"

"Call me Ryan, Ms. Pierce." I shrug. "I don't know. Just something about you strikes me as dangerous."

She bursts out laughing.

"What's so funny?"

"That's kind of my nickname."

"I bet it was well-earned, too," I say with a smile.

Tourists circle us, standing there in the middle of the boardwalk, still shaking hands, gazes locked. Screams fill the air as the roller coaster rockets past and the buzz of the world around us slowly falls away in a blur of sound and light.

All I can see is Fallon. It's like an electrical current keeps our hands stuck together.

"Excuse me," a voice says and a shoulder bumps

me out of my reverie.

We release hands at the same time and I take an unsteady step back as the outside world comes rushing back.

"So, you have a knack for hacking, huh?" she says and starts walking again.

"Do you approve?"

"It's one of those necessary evils." She takes another bite of her churro. "Especially in my line of work."

"Which is?"

"I work for a security company."

"Private security? Like bodyguard type stuff?"

"That's one of our specialties at Slater Security."

I arch a brow. She's so cagey. "What else does Fallon and Slater Security specialize in? Besides avoiding my questions."

"I'm not avoiding your questions," she says.

"You just don't give much detail," I amend. "And I'm a detail-oriented kinda guy."

"Really?" she asks in a blasé tone.

"Not my fault, though," I say and tap a finger against my head. "Photographic memory."

Fallon stops up short and turns to face me, full of curiosity. *"Really?"*

Finally, I've snagged her interest. "Yep." This time I leave her hanging and walk to the edge of the boardwalk. We've made it all the way to the end and I lean my arms on the railing and gaze out over the gray Pacific Ocean.

She sidles up next to me and props a hip against the rail. "So you remember everything you see and never forget it?"

"Not exactly."

"How does it work, exactly?"

"I'll see something and remember it down to the most finite detail. It'll usually stick in my brain for a few months, but it does eventually fade."

"That's incredible."

I shrug. "Made school easy."

"You must've passed med school with flying

colors."

"I did. But it wasn't for me."

"So you said. Why not?"

"I hate blood and guts. The moment they cut that cadaver open, I didn't know if I was going to puke or pass out."

She grimaces. "Yeah, gory stuff really isn't my jam either. Unfortunately, I saw quite a bit of it while deployed."

Ah-ha. "You're military?" Suddenly Fallon makes a lot more sense to me– the secretiveness, the calluses, her job and that tough exterior she wears like armor.

"Special Forces," she says vaguely.

"Really? Can you talk about it?"

"I was Delta Force for almost ten years," she says, gauging my reaction.

"No shit! They're like the meanest and baddest motherfu- guys out there. Only a handful of women make Task Force Green."

"There are a few of us. But you're right. Barely

any."

"I've played video games, but you've done the real thing. You know how cool that is?"

"That doesn't intimidate you?" she asks.

"Hell no. It's intriguing. Makes me want to know more about you." It makes me want to see if I can soften those sharp edges of hers, too. She doesn't say anything and an odd look crosses her face. *Disbelief maybe?* "Well, thank you for your service. That's an outstanding achievement."

She shrugs it off and crumples the churro wrapper up. "It was exciting while it lasted."

"Do you miss it?"

"I do. My life is pretty boring nowadays."

The moment the words are out of her mouth, someone steps up behind us and I see Fallon's body tense and eyes go wide. My gaze dips to see a gun jammed in her lower back.

"Gimme the card," a huge man growls. He's the size of a damn linebacker and the gun in his meaty hand should probably trigger my fight or flight response. Instead, I stand there, completely frozen.

I have no idea what the hell to do when suddenly Fallon shoves an elbow into his gut and sidesteps in one of the quickest moves I've ever seen. She spins and slams her palm underneath his chin and his head snaps back.

"Ryan, run!" she yells.

But it's like I'm glued to the spot and all I can do is watch Fallon throw a series of punches. She blocks the attacker's fists and moves so fast it makes me dizzy.

"Go!" she orders me again.

I nod and turn, jogging away from the chaos when a motorcycle comes screeching out of nowhere. People scream and scatter as the bike spins in a half-circle, smoke rising from the peeling rubber, and leaves black marks on the planks. The engine revs, tires squeal and the driver heads straight toward me.

Oh, shit, I think. *This can't be good.*

Chapter Seven: Fallon

When I see the motorcycle barreling down on Ryan, my stomach clenches and I race toward him, throwing myself into him. We land hard with a thud, roll across the planks and the motorcycle roars past our heads, barely missing.

"C'mon! Up!" I yell. Ryan looks a little dazed and I yank him back as two more bikers appear. *Fuck.* "Get over there!" I shove him toward an alcove and concentrate on the first bike headed toward me. Just before it reaches me, I jump out of its way and then leap onto the back of the bike, punching the driver hard enough in his kidney to make him piss blood for the next two days. He yelps, we skid sideways, tilt and go down hard.

The driver is wearing a helmet so I can't hit his face. But I can steal his ride. Ripping the handlebars away, I haul the metal monster up and throw a leg over the seat. Revving the gas, I spin the bike around in a 180-degree squeal, and spot Ryan.

"Ryan, c'mon!" I yell and he hustles forward. "Get on!"

As Ryan jumps on the back, I take off, and catch a glimpse of my black suitcase in the side mirror. *Fuck.* As much as I want my gear, there's nothing I can do about it now. Instead, I focus on driving us away from the ocean and toward land. There are a million people on this damn boardwalk, though, and I'm weaving through the crowd, doing my best to avoid hitting anyone.

Glancing over my shoulder, I see two bikes following us and curse. "Hang on tight!" I yell. We're almost off the boardwalk and dodging through the final stretch of screaming tourists. When we hit the sidewalk, I gun it and the bike flies forward. We leap the curb, land in the street and barely avoid crashing into a car. A cacophony of horns pierce the air as cars swerve to avoid us and each other.

I need to get us out of traffic and all this congestion, but this is downtown Santa Monica and that just isn't going to happen. I speed up and a glance in the mirror lets me know that both tangoes are still in hot pursuit.

At the next street, I take a hard right and we nearly tip over. "Ryan! Lean into the curves with me!"

"How the hell am I supposed to know when you're turning?" he yells back above the wind and the engine. "Not like you're using your blinker!"

"Oh, shut up and hold on!" His arms tighten around my waist as we zoom up Third Street. "Shit," I hiss. Probably wasn't the best decision to turn here, right in the middle of the Third Street Promenade. Traffic isn't allowed on the road; it's closed to cars because of the high volume of shoppers.

Motorcycles, on the other hand, fit right through the cement blockade and I speed through tourist central, doing my best to stay ahead of the bad guys, not lose Ryan off the back and look for an opportunity to shake these assholes.

"You almost hit that guy!" Ryan yells.

Oops. I glance in the side mirror and he's fine. Pissed maybe, but alright. "Almost doesn't count," I say.

We zigzag around palm trees, benches and shoppers for another minute and then I finally spot what I'm looking for– the entrance to a parking garage. "Turning!" I inform Ryan in a smartass tone. We take the turn far too fast, nearly spilling off the bike. Luckily, Ryan leans with me this time and we make it.

I burn rubber up the ramp and keep going higher. "Get ready," I say. "We're about to ditch these guys."

After we careen around the next curve, putting the tangoes chasing us temporarily out of view, I drive straight through the open stairwell door.

"What the hell are you doing?" Ryan demands, tightening his arms around me.

"Going back down," I say. The bike hits the steps and down we go. THUMP, THUMP THUMP! When we hit the landing, I guide us down the next set of stairs and then we burst out the back door into an alley.

"You're insane," Ryan says, mouth near my ear, arms wrapped tightly around me.

It hits me hard that I really like the feel of him pressing against my back. His chest is hard, firmer than I would've guessed, and it feels good to be encased in his muscled arms.

It's been a long time since I was in a man's embrace.

"Are we going back to get our suitcases?"

"It's too dangerous." I really want my gear, but I can't take the chance that one of the bad guys might be waiting for us. Instead, I turn the bike toward Beverly Hills. "We're going back to my hotel."

We need to lay low after this and I make sure no one is following us on the drive back. Calling Dash and stashing the card in my pocket somewhere secure are my main priorities.

Luckily, we don't get pulled over for driving around without helmets and I ditch the bike early. We take an Uber the rest of the way back to the hotel because I'm not taking any chances when it comes to potential GPS trackers. Nowadays almost every vehicle has one.

When we arrive at The Beverly Hills Hotel, Ryan looks impressed. "Wow," he murmurs, eyeing the endless palm trees lining the drive and the iconic pink building with its green sign. "This place is legendary. They used to call it "The Pink Palace." Did you know when it opened in 1912, it was the only place for miles and surrounded by lima bean farms?"

I pause as we walk up the red carpet beneath the green and white striped awning. "How do you know-" I look over into his intelligent brown eyes. "Ah, the photographic memory strikes."

His mouth edges up. "I read a book about the hotel before I came out here. It has quite a history. Richard Burton and Elizabeth Taylor honeymooned in a bungalow here. And Marilyn Monroe's favorite was Bungalow 1. If you have $8500 to burn, we could spend the night there."

A warmth fills my lower belly at the idea of spending the night with Ryan. "Yeah, well, I'm not really into the Hollywood scene," I say, trying to sound nonchalant and not think about what that night in Bungalow 1 would be like with him.

"There's so much history here," he continues as a bellman opens the door for us.

"C'mon. Our suite is this way."

When we reach the room, there's no sign of Sierra. I notice a note on the desk, swipe it up and read Sierra's bubbly handwriting.

"She went to the pool. Let's go down and make

sure she's okay."

"Why wouldn't she be? And who were those men chasing us?" He crosses his arms. "You know, don't you?"

I shake my head. "Not exactly. Look, I'll explain everything later. Right now, I want to make sure Sierra is secure."

We head back down to the lobby and Mr. Photographic Memory starts giving me a tour. "The marble floors and chandelier are from Italy," he says. Halfway down the grand staircase, he points at the huge floor to ceiling windows. "When they built the hotel, they made sure each room would receive sunlight at some point during the day. Cool, huh?"

God, he is such a geek and, for some inexplicable reason, I really like it. *I like him.* I run a hand through my hair and listen to him babble as we walk outside. A ray of sunshine hits his dark brown eyes just right and they seem to glimmer. I clear my throat and kind of wish he was wearing his sexy glasses.

"Hey, look!" he exclaims and starts walking toward a little playground.

"I think the pool is that way," I say, but he ignores me and heads over to the swings. Shaking my head, I follow him and he grabs the chains, holding the seat steady.

"Hop on," he says.

I laugh and cross my arms. "No thanks."

"C'mon, why not?"

My smile fades when I realize he's serious and I look around, but we're all alone. No kids or parents in sight. I lean closer and mock-whisper, "Because I'm not five."

His dark gaze locks with mine. "I dare you."

Narrowing my eyes, I can't miss the challenge in his voice and there's nothing I love more than pushing myself out of my comfort zone. Besides, he threw the gauntlet down and now I can't refuse. I lower myself into the swing and Ryan pulls me back in a fast move that sets my heart thumping. He lifts me up until my back is against his chest. Suspended there, legs dangling, I get a whiff of his clean scent when he leans in and says, "Hold on tight."

My stomach flutters at the close contact. Then he pulls me up even higher and releases the swing with a big push. A squeal erupts from my throat as I go flying forward, boots lifting up against the blazing blue sky.

Tendrils pull free from my ponytail as I swing backwards and Ryan gives me another push. As I go back and forth, higher and higher, I automatically pump my legs and let myself enjoy the moment. It's freeing, and that's something I haven't felt in a very long time.

Eventually, I slow down and drag my feet to stop myself. Ryan catches the chains and hauls me to a complete stop. I look up at him and his smile is contagious. "It's been a while since I've done that," I say.

"What about that?" he asks and nods at the slide.

"Probably even longer."

He motions for me to follow him and I can't believe that I do. But I'm not planning on actually climbing up the ladder and sliding down. I'm just humoring him.

"After you," Ryan says.

"No way."

"Embrace your inner child. I get the feeling you don't let her loose nearly enough."

"That's because I'm an adult with

responsibilities."

"You don't let yourself play?" he asks and cocks his head to the side.

Again, I hear that challenge in his voice. "I play," I assure him and place a hand on my hip.

"So, play with me."

I'm not exactly sure what this conversation is about anymore and get the distinct impression it's veering off into dangerous territory. I pull my gaze away from his and my mouth edges up. "Okay, fine," I say and start up the ladder.

Ryan follows close behind and some wicked part of me adds an extra swivel to my hips. I know my ass is practically at his eye level. When I reach the top, I sit down and look over my shoulder where he stands right behind me. The heat flickering in his espresso eyes makes my belly tighten.

"See you at the bottom." I push off and glide down.

Ryan slides down a moment later and I pop up and dart out of the way before he runs into me.

"Better watch where you're going, Mercer," I

say. He stands, forcing me to look up at him. It's easy to forget how tall he is until he's towering over me.

"How do you feel about the spinner?" he asks and tilts his head toward the low playground equipment that's famous for sending kids flying off in every direction as it ramps up to warp speed.

"It's dangerous…so I love it."

"Let's go for a ride then."

I don't hesitate and hop up on the metal merry-go-round. I drop down in a crouch and grab hold of the bars.

Ryan starts walking, turning it as he moves in a circle. "Are you ready?"

"I'm always ready."

He smirks and then launches into a sprint, making the world around me spin hard. Gravity tries to pull me off, but I drop down on my butt and wrap my arms and legs around the bar in front of me. Ryan jumps on next to me and we both wind up on our backs, hanging on for dear life. My body slides against his and I yelp as the power of his spin seems to go on and on.

The trees and sky turn madly above me and I let myself enjoy the moment. By the time we stop spinning, my shoulders are shaking with laughter. I can't remember the last time I felt this spontaneous and uninhibited. Ryan is bringing out a light, playful side of me that I honestly thought had died a long time ago.

"That was fun," I say a little breathlessly, my arm pressing against his warm, muscular one.

"*You're* fun," he says and turns his head to look at me. "When you're not being all mysterious and dangerous."

"Gotta keep up appearances when I work for Dash Slater." I sit up and glance over through the trees, toward the pool.

"Just don't forget to let loose every once in a while."

I hop off the spinner and brush off the back of my black jeans. "Yes, sir," I say, feeling frisky.

"I like your playful side," Ryan says.

I'm not sure how to respond to that so instead I point in the direction of the pool. "I need to check on Sierra. Are you coming with me?"

Ryan nods and we head toward the pool. He starts telling me about all of the famous people who have swam in it. As we walk through the Citrus Garden– that's what he calls it– he starts talking about the private upper and lower level cabanas that surround the pool.

"There are 52 phone lines out here," he says with a grin.

"Why do they need that many phones when everyone has a cell?"

"Because, dahling," he drawls in a silly, pretentious accent. "If you aren't paged at The Beverly Hills Hotel, you're simply nobody."

I burst out laughing and, for the first time in a long time, I let myself relax and just enjoy the moment. He's so playful and laidback– the complete opposite of me. He's right. It feels nice to loosen up a bit. Normally I'm wound a little too tight, especially while on a job.

For whatever reason, Ryan reminds me of an anchor, stable and secure, even in the midst of a storm. I've weathered my share of tempests so a reliable and steady shoulder to lean on is nice. And new for me. I rarely lean on anyone. Ever.

We step out of the garden and my gaze darts around the pool. "There she is," I say and nod toward Sierra. She's wearing a tiny, pink and white polka dot bikini and lays stretched out on a lounge chair, face hidden beneath a large-brimmed hat and sunglasses. The beefy ex-cop who I slipped a few hundred bucks to earlier gives me a discreet nod and then disappears.

The moment she notices us, she sits up and waves. "Ryan! It's so nice to see you again. Sit." She pats the space beside her and a jealous streak sizzles through me when he sits next to her. "Are you guys okay? You look windblown."

I brush the loose wisps of hair off my face with a self-conscious hand. "We had a run-in with some tangoes and a bumpy ride."

"Ooh, tangoes? That's military-speak for the enemy," she informs Ryan.

Sierra Simone may say the most idiotic things but she does it in such a charming way that it makes her irresistible. She has an innocent allure about her that you can't help but like. Even when jealousy makes you want to hate her.

She's also everything that I'm not– feminine, artless, sweet and drop-dead gorgeous. Flirty banter comes as easily to her as breathing and I have no idea how to properly flirt. It's not something I've ever needed in the field so I never took the time to learn and cultivate it. Maybe I should have, I realize, when I hear Ryan laugh at something she just whispered in his ear.

Bristling, I bite down on the inside of my cheek. "I need to call the office," I say and spin around. I'm not sure either one of them hears or cares. Yanking my phone out of my jacket pocket, I disappear back into the Citrus Garden, pull up Dash Slater and hit send.

"Hey, Fallon," his deep, smooth voice says. "How's the job going?"

"Totally FUBAR, Dash," I grumble and pluck a leaf off an orange tree.

"What happened?"

"It seems Sierra Simone has the combination to a safe somewhere in Bel Air that holds a priceless ruby necklace, specifically Cupid's Bow. And now someone wants to steal it from her."

"You gotta be kidding me?"

"So far today, I've been hijacked by a fake driver, got in a fist fight and just escaped some bad guys in a motorcycle chase through the Third Street

Promenade. Oh, yeah, and my suitcase got mixed up with someone else's and I have zero weapons."

"Anything else?" he asks, voice dry and slightly amused.

"Yeah, as a matter of fact, Miss Perfect Sierra is driving me crazy and somewhere along the way we picked up some random tourist and he keeps showing up like a bad rash."

"He?"

"Ryan Mercer. He's the one who accidentally took my luggage and we were in the process of swapping it back when the bad guys interrupted us."

"And Ryan is with you right now?"

"He's currently sitting poolside and giggling with Sierra."

Silence fills the line. Then, Dash says, "Do I detect a note of jealousy, Pierce?"

I practically choke. "What?" I sputter. "You know me, Dash. I don't get jealous."

"No, not usually. But I get the feeling that Sierra and Ryan 'giggling' is bothering you."

"I don't care what they do," I snap. Far too quickly. *Dammit.* I know I just gave myself away. Not like I could keep anything secret from Dash Slater for long, anyway, though. The man can smell BS a mile away. Or, in this case, 120 miles away. He's got quite the infallible bullshit detector.

"You're cute, Dangerous," he says, voice teasing. "In your own, stubborn and annoying way, of course. If you like this guy, go put on a bathing suit and pull up a lounge chair. He'd be lucky you made the effort."

I huff out an indignant scoff. "You're joking, right? I'm working."

"You're allowed breaks."

"Take your own advice, Slater," I say more harshly than I intend. Dash is a workaholic and we all know it at the office.

"Touché. Alright, where's the necklace again?"

"Stashed in a safe and I've got the combination in my pocket."

Dash swears under his breath. "What do you want to do? I see three options: remain in L.A. and continue to handle the op on your own; stay put and I send backup; or bring Sierra down here where it's safest."

"I think we should get the necklace and come down to San Diego until her prince can pick her up. But, she's not going to be happy about that scenario since her fashion show is in two days."

"Prince?"

"Yeah. Didn't I mention she's dating European royalty?"

Dash chuckles. Then his mood swiftly alters. "Ah, hell. I gotta go. Aidan is down in the holding cell and just pulled a taser on Veronica. I'm adding this to Cullen's bill. Keep me posted."

So Aidan "Vain" Wolf is still trying to pry information from Veronica's brightly-painted lips through any means necessary. *Interesting.* Not like she doesn't deserve it. That's what happens when you try to turn a bunch of former SEALs into mindless super soldiers that you want to use for all kinds of messed up reasons. What did she expect would happen? They're gonna fight back. Project Phoenix should have stayed buried. Trying to reactivate Aidan and his teammates was a bad deal. I'm kinda glad he's making her pay for it.

"Roger." We disconnect and I hear Sierra's

tinkling laughter all the way over here. Gritting my teeth, I try not to let it bother me.

But, for some reason, it's like nails scraping down a chalkboard.

Grr.

Chapter Eight: Ryan

Sierra invites me to join her and Fallon for dinner at the iconic Polo Lounge and there's no way I'm saying no. Any excuse to spend more time staring at Fallon Pierce works for me. Sierra is sweet and all, but Fallon is on an entirely different level that intrigues, attracts and mystifies me.

Sierra tells me her fashion show is still a couple of days away and I have the urge to change my hotel accommodations. Sure, staying at this swanky place is going to cost a small fortune, but this is a once in a lifetime opportunity for me. And anything that keeps me close to Fallon, I'm grabbing. I mention it to Sierra and she claps excitedly.

"I don't want to look like a stalker," I say.

"Oh, no! It'll be fun! Trust me, you aren't a stalker. And I should know because I have one." She winks at me.

Okay, I'm convinced. After a quick call to the hotel in Santa Monica to cancel my reservations, I find myself in the large lobby booking a room here. I don't want to know the price as I slide my credit card across the counter.

Hell, I'm on vacation, right? I may as well make it one to remember.

After checking out my new digs, I call my buddy Joe to let him know I switched hotels. I can't help but brag a little about my current situation– I mean, how often do you get tangled up with a supermodel *and* Lara Croft?

Right now, it's really good to be me and I'm going to enjoy every moment while it lasts. Sierra told me to meet them in an hour and I desperately need some clothes since my suitcase is still sitting on the Santa Monica Pier. There's no way I can walk into the world-famous Polo Lounge in these grubby-looking jeans.

I read about the men's store tucked away in the

basement level here at the hotel so I make sure I have my credit card and head over. It's owned by an Iranian-born, former fashion model named Amir and I distinctly remember the insane prices mentioned, but I don't really have a choice. There's no time to go anywhere else and where would I go anyway? Rodeo Drive? *Because, yeah, that would be a lot cheaper.*

The place's motto is "understated elegance," but I'm just hoping to get a pair of pants and a shirt for under five grand. Twenty minutes later, my mission is nearly accomplished when my eye is drawn to a leather jacket that the owner immediately slides off the hanger and helps me slip on. And, damn, it fits like a glove. The leather feels like butter and I turn in front of the mirror.

As stupid as it sounds, I feel cool in it. I also have an overwhelming need to impress Fallon. Glancing down at the price tag, I try not to grimace. Okay, so this 30-minute shopping spree is going to nearly max out my entire line of credit.

But you know what? I'm in Beverly Hills and I have a gorgeous woman I want to awe and amaze.

"Let's do it, Amir," I say and hand my credit card over. The damn thing is practically smoking, but one more glance in the mirror and I know it's a splurge worth taking.

No more t-shirts with geeky sayings, I think, and look down at my slim-fitted black pants, white shirt and leather jacket.

The moment I step out of the store, my cell phone buzzes. I don't recognize the number, but answer it, anyway. "Hello?"

"Is this Ryan Mercer?" a man asks.

"Yes."

"My name's Mike and I found your suitcase on the boardwalk."

"Really?" I'm happy, but at the same time, I just dropped almost two months' salary on the new outfit I'm wearing. Something tells me this edgier look might make Fallon notice me while my Star Wars t-shirt probably wouldn't. "Thanks for calling. I thought that thing was lost forever. There didn't happen to be another one by it, was there?" I ask, wondering if he has Fallon's case, too.

"Sure was," Mike says. "Tag says it belongs to Fallon-"

"Pierce," I finish. "Yep, that's the one. I can pick

them up in an hour or so if that's alright?"

"Well, where are you? I'm going to be out, but if I'm in the neighborhood of wherever you are, I can drop them off."

This is where I should've gotten suspicious. But nope. "I'm staying at The Beverly Hills Hotel," I blurt out.

"Hey, what're the chances? I'm going to be passing right by there. I'll drop them off with the concierge."

"Are you sure? I can meet you-"

"It's not a problem. Happy to do it."

"Thanks a lot."

After hanging up, I head over to the Polo Lounge and I feel like a million bucks. Well, hell, I should after dropping a small fortune with Amir. I took extra time to style my hair in that perfectly-messy look and I didn't shave, hoping the stubble gives me an edgier look. I just hope I don't appear desperate. Snagging Fallon's attention has quickly become my top priority and suddenly it doesn't seem like such a shot in the dark anymore.

Earlier, when we were out by the pool, she almost seemed jealous. As sweet as Sierra is, I'm only interested in the ebony-haired badass who's stirring things up in me that I've never felt for any woman before.

The moment I walk into the lounge, I spot them at a table and make my way over.

"Ryan!" Sierra gushes. "Come sit here by me."

I glance over at Fallon and she's looking at me with the strangest expression on her face. I can't tell if it's good or bad.

"You look fantastic," Sierra says, running a hand down the sleeve of my jacket. "So handsome. Right, Fallon?"

Instead of answering, Fallon takes a sip of her water.

Too late, though. I saw the flash of interest light up those aquamarine eyes before she averted her gaze. My mouth edges up as I sit down beside Sierra and a wave of confidence fills me. Even though I'm closer to Sierra logistics-wise, I'm in the perfect position because I'm directly across from Fallon and I have nowhere else to focus except her beautiful face.

"I think we should leave tomorrow and go to San Diego," Fallon says. "Slater Security is the safest place for you right now until your boyfriend can pick you up."

I can't help but notice the way she emphasizes the word boyfriend and I hide a smile.

"No!" Sierra cries. "I'm walking in the biggest show of my career in two days. There's no way I'm leaving now."

"Sierra, it's not safe here. Someone is after that necklace and they're not going to back down until they get it," Fallon says.

"Then do your job and protect me," Sierra says matter of factly.

"I need my gear," Fallon reminds her, an exasperated edge to her voice.

"Oh, someone named Mike called me," I say. "He's got our luggage and is going to drop it off."

"What?" Fallon's eyes narrow.

"Said he found it on the boardwalk."

"A Good Samaritan!" Sierra exclaims. "That's so nice."

"I thought so," I say and Fallon frowns without comment.

"Ryan, let's get you a drink." Sierra grabs a passing waiter.

"Who wants your necklace?" I ask and turn to Sierra.

"Long story short, I'm dating a prince and he gave me the combination to the safe that holds my birthday gift which is a really expensive ruby necklace and now some thieves are after it. Do you want to order a bottle of champagne?"

She says everything in a run-on sentence and so nonchalantly that I chuckle. "You don't seem too concerned."

"I'm not," Sierra says and sucks down the rest of her Cosmopolitan. "Fallon has the combination, so it's safe."

I turn my attention to Fallon. "You memorized it?"

Fallon shakes her head and discreetly removes a card from the inside pocket of her leather jacket. She slides it across the table to me. "That's from her princely boyfriend."

I can't help but smile at her snarky tone as I pick up the card and open it. "Do you mind?" I ask Sierra.

"Nope," she assures me, too busy trying to pluck a cherry from her drink.

I skim over what's clearly a love letter and when I reach the end, I see the string of letters, numbers and symbols: *T6@pG924M6d&+q/?20OL0(K)ChF+KD*. "This opens the safe?" Fallon nods as I hand the card back. "Then you should destroy it."

"How would I get the safe open then?" Sierra asks.

I tap my temple. "I'll remember it."

"Your photographic memory," Fallon says under her breath.

"Yep," I say and toss her a wink.

A flush stains her cheeks and our gazes lock. I don't know what's going on, but she's looking at me in a way she hasn't before. There's heat in the depths of her eyes and when she licks her lips my groin tightens.

A Frank Sinatra song starts and I stand up. "Dance with me?"

When I offer Fallon my hand, she looks up at me

like I've lost my mind. Sierra giggles and pops the cherry into her mouth.

"I don't dance," Fallon says just like I knew she would.

"Well, I do. So you can take a break and I'll lead, boss."

Hesitation fills her and I waggle my fingers.

"Aww, go dance with him," Sierra says.

Just when I think she's going to refuse me again, she slowly places her hand in mine and I pull her up. My smile is ridiculously huge as I lead her over to the dance floor.

A few couples sway on the polished floor and Fallon tenses.

"Maybe you should've asked Sierra," she says.

"I don't want to dance with Sierra." I pull her closer. My arm wraps around her lower back and my left hand curls around her right one. Our bodies are close but not quite touching, and she swallows hard.

"I hope you have very low expectations when it comes to my dancing skills."

I step back and shake her arms out. "Relax." Then I tug her back into my arms, flush against me, and spin us toward the right side of the dance floor. Her leg moves between mine and despite all the self-deprecation, she keeps up just fine. "Are you holding out on me?"

"What do you mean?" she asks.

"You're very graceful. You might dance just as well as you drive a motorcycle."

She chuckles. "Definitely not."

"This is a great song," I say.

She looks up at me with amusement glittering in those aquamarine eyes. "Are you joking?"

"If you tell me you don't like Sinatra, we're going to have a serious problem."

"I didn't realize anyone under 60 listens to him," she teases.

I pretend to scowl then drop her in a dip. She laughs and I pull her back up. "My grandpa loved Sinatra. My grandparents practically raised me because my parents were always working. After school, I'd go straight to their house. Did my homework, ate dinner and then sat on the front porch with my grandpa. He always had Francis playing on his little, busted-up radio."

"Francis?"

"Francis Albert Sinatra, aka ol' Blue Eyes."

"That's sweet."

"What about you? Who were you close to growing up?"

A cloud flits over her pretty face and the mood plummets. *Shit.* I get the feeling I just asked the worst possible question.

"My parents," she finally says in a low voice. "I'm an only child so we were very close. But they died."

Fuck. I'm such a dumbass. "I'm sorry. Have they been gone long?"

"Since I was 16." She almost looks surprised that the words are coming out of her mouth. That she's confiding in me. "After they passed, I lived with a distant cousin for a couple of years. Then I turned 18 and joined the military. And the rest is history."

The song ends and she pulls back.

"Thanks for the dance."

And just like that, Fallon is history, too.

I squeeze my eyes shut and inwardly curse. Well, I screwed that up royally. *Idiot.* Following her back to the table, I can't help but wish that played out differently. Once we're sitting again, Sierra's gaze moves back and forth between us. She's far from subtle and I take a drink of water as the waiter arrives with our food.

"So there's no way to convince you to skip the fashion show?" Fallon asks.

"Nope," Sierra says and takes a bite of salad.

Fallon shoves a hand through her long hair. "Okay. Then I need backup from my team."

"I can help," I blurt out. "Whatever you need."

Fallon bursts out laughing and I frown.

"What's so funny?" I ask.

"You're a civilian. What do you know about private security? This isn't a joke. Sierra's life could be on the line and I need more than a guy with a suitcase full of geeky t-shirts. I need competent and trained professionals."

Wow. That stings.

"It's sweet of you to offer, though, Ryan," Sierra says and touches my arm. "But Fallon is right. We should probably let the badasses handle it."

"Yeah, sure," I say, miffed at Fallon for assuming I'm useless when it comes to anything physical. "What the hell do I know about private security? Being an idiot civilian and all."

Fallon tilts her head. "That's not what I meant."

"Sure you did." And it's not just that she said it. She laughed. I guess it takes more than a leather jacket to be respected. Suddenly I feel like such a poser. *I wonder if I can return these stupid, over-priced clothes?*

I'm insulted and I feel like a fool. I really misinterpreted things with Fallon. I thought there was some chemistry sparking between us, but I guess not. *Whatever.* It's no surprise that the geek doesn't get the girl.

I order another martini or whatever it is I'm drinking and decide to drown my sorrows. Instead of dwelling on Fallon, I flirt it up with Sierra and we order that bottle of champagne. Her smiles and witty banter pick up my deflated mood and bruised ego. Of course, the alcohol helps, too, and by the end of dinner, I can't stop laughing.

"Should we order dessert?" Sierra asks.

"None for me," Fallon says and throws her napkin on the table.

She's been acting pissy for the last half of the meal and I'm trying not to pay too much attention to her. It's damn hard, though. She lights up the freaking room even when she's glowering.

"Let's go back up to the room then. Ryan, are you coming?"

"Uh, sure," I say. The whole way up, Sierra hangs on my arm and it's clear she's had too much to drink.

When we turn down the hallway to their suite, I see the concierge with our suitcases. *Perfect timing.*

"Thank God," Fallon murmurs and reaches for hers.

We thank him and Fallon unlocks the suite, pulling her case with her. I roll mine in, too, then Sierra tugs me toward her room. I glance over my shoulder at Fallon who watches us like a hawk. She gives us both a sour look before she turns and stomps toward her room.

"C'mon," Sierra says, dragging me into her bedroom and nudging the door shut. She gives me the eye and sashays over, running a finger down my chest. "Do you know how cute you are?"

Okay, so here's that rare moment that happens once in a lifetime– my chance to sleep with a supermodel. Only problem is I can't stop thinking about how much I wish Sierra was Fallon. When she cups my face, I pull back.

"I really like you," I say. "But…"

Sierra grins. "You like her better."

Am I that transparent?

"It's okay," Sierra says. "I kind of figured from the way you two were staring at each other all night. Besides, I have Armand. I'm just feeling lonely and tipsy."

"She was staring at me?"

Sierra smiles. "Oh, yeah. Majorly. You know what I think?"

"What?"

"I think you should march your cute little butt across the living room and seduce that battle-hardened babe."

"Um-"

"No ums, Ryan, unless it's the moaning kind. Now go stick your tongue down her throat and-"

A loud crash cuts her off and we both freeze.

"What was that?" Sierra whispers, eyes widening.

I shrug and right as I reach for the door handle, a boot kicks it in. BAM! The door flies inward and I see two men in black ski masks holding guns.

Chapter Nine: Fallon

I close my door and even though I'm happy to have my weapons back, I can't stop thinking about how Sierra just dragged Ryan into her room. They both were drinking too much and are probably going at it right now.

My gut clenches and I hate thinking about it. Maybe I should've been nicer to Ryan at dinner, but jealousy got the best of me. When that happens, I can turn snippy fast. I shouldn't have laughed when he offered to help and realized too late that I hurt his feelings.

God, why is he so damn sensitive? He's worse than a little girl.

I grab my black case that I thought was gone forever, unlock it and check to make sure everything is present and accounted for. Luckily, it all looks good. I pull out my backpack, unzip it and check the cord I use when I do a short jump off a building. Short means less than 20 floors. It's such a rush stepping off a roof or out a window and gliding down to the pavement. Kind of my signature move, if I do say so myself.

It's weird but that same rush came over me tonight when I saw Ryan walk into the restaurant. *Holy hell.* Gone was the dorky t-shirt and in its place was that yummy black leather jacket. Who knew he'd look so good in leather?

Most of the men I've dated have that same military-short haircut. But Ryan's brown hair, though shorter on the sides, is longer and perfectly-mussed on top. I've had the urge to run my fingers through it several times and I'm doing my best to ignore how cute it is. We actually had a moment there in the beginning when we were dancing and then he and Sierra began to flirt up a storm.

I'm not sure why I even care. Ryan Mercer is not my type whatsoever. He's easygoing, sweet and wouldn't harm a fly. We're complete opposites in every way. Though when I think back over my dating life, I've only been out with the same kind of men–alpha assholes.

And that's never worked out for me.

Maybe it's time to try something new because the track I'm currently on is leading me nowhere fast. But he likes Sierra and I can't blame him. While she's willowy, blonde and charming, I'm so far from that it's comical.

As I'm trying to convince myself that I don't care about Ryan, I hear a crash in the living room followed by what sounds like a low thud. *What the hell?* I grab my Glock 19, feeling comfort in its familiar weight, and open my door.

The last thing I expect to see is several men dressed all in black, their faces covered.

Fuck. They're here for the safe combination and they're not even trying to be sneaky about it. Their boldness catches me off-guard for about two seconds. Unfortunately, that's all it takes for the closest mercenary to turn and fire off a shot at me.

I must be off my game because I throw myself out of the bullet's path a moment too late. A stinging sensation rips across my upper arm, but I ignore it and dive behind the bed for cover as the merc steps into the doorway. *Just a nick*, I tell myself. I've had much worse injuries in the field.

"What's the combination?" he demands.

How the hell did they find us? I was so careful.

I peer over the edge of the bed and shoot. When he swears and steps out of sight, I waste no time and launch myself toward the balcony doors. The nights get cool here in February and I'm not surprised by the chilly air that hits me.

I registered Sierra and I under fake names. I made sure to ditch the SUV miles from here. I even-

Oh, fucking hell.

The bad guys were the ones who called Ryan. Why didn't I catch on earlier? I knew something didn't feel right when he told us at dinner. *Ugh.* I've been too preoccupied with thoughts of him and Sierra that I missed the obvious. *God, I'm an idiot.*

Pistol up and held close to my body, I hurry forward. Luckily, our balcony is a long one that extends from my bedroom past the living room and down to Sierra's room. Knowing I don't have much time before the thug follows me out here, I haul ass over to the opposite side and pause, back pressed against the wall.

A glimpse inside allows me to quickly assess the situation: two armed tangoes and the shorter one has his Ruger pointed in Ryan's face. *Oh, God.* He's not trained to handle this kind of situation and I see him talking when he needs to shut the hell up.

When I hear the merc step out onto the balcony from my room, I realize it's time to crash this party. I kick the double doors open and aim my Glock at the asshole with his gun on Ryan. Sierra screams and the taller man points his gun at her while the other merc moves up behind me.

I spin, kicking the gun out of his grip, and it hits the floor and clatters away. He lunges toward me and I dodge to the side and pistol-whip him across the face. As he staggers, blood pouring from his broken nose, the shorter man orders me to drop my weapon.

"Enough! Or he's dead," the thug booms.

My gaze jumps over to Ryan and the first thing that hits me is he doesn't look scared. Unlike Sierra who's shaking like a leaf. In fact, he is pissed and I realize that his attention is on my arm. I glance down and see bright red blood staining my shirt but ignore it.

"Where's the combination?" the man asks. "Give

it to us now or they both die."

"It's not here," Ryan blurts out.

"Shut up, Ryan," I hiss.

Our gazes clash. I don't need him playing hero and I hope the cold look I give him conveys that thought.

"He's right," Sierra says, piping in, voice wavering. "I put it in a safe deposit box at the bank."

I get that they're trying to stall, but this isn't going to end well.

"You dumb bitch," the man says and waves his gun. "Now you're going to make this way more difficult than it has to be. Tie them up," he orders and nods at me and Ryan.

"Gimme that," the first merc rips my Glock away while the other one pulls out a length of rope.

He ties my wrists up followed by Ryan's. "Sit down," the taller thug snaps. "On the floor, back to back."

I'm going to get us out of this, but I need to make it look like we're cooperating so they let their guards down. I exchange a look with Ryan. I want him to know everything is going to be okay and he seems to understand my telepathic reassurance. We turn and sit down, backs pressed against each other.

The mercenary wraps the rope around the both of us and ties it off in a sloppy knot. I sit forward a little without it being too noticeable and hope I've created enough space so I'll be able to get out of the bindings quickly.

After securing us, the shorter thug grabs Sierra's arm and yanks her toward the door. Before they leave, he glares at me over his beefy shoulder. "I suggest you stay here until she gives us the combination. Otherwise, she's dead." He shoves his gun into Sierra's side and she whimpers.

I clench my jaw as they leave and know that I need to get untied fast before I lose them. Letting them hurt Sierra or get their hands on the ruby necklace is not going to happen on my watch.

"Are we going after her?" Ryan asks.

I start tugging at the rope around my wrists, working it loose. "I'm going after her," I correct him.

"I can help."

"I think you've already done enough," I say.

"What do you mean?"

"That was your Good Samaritan Mike."

"Oh, shit," he mumbles.

I'm trying really hard not to roll my eyes or sigh. After realizing how sensitive he is, I don't want to hurt his feelings again. I'm still pulling on my bindings when I feel the rope around us begin to loosen and slide down my chest.

"Are you-"

"I'm free," he says.

How in the world did he get free so fast? I wonder. The thought barely finishes running through my head when the rope tied around the both of us falls down onto my lap.

"How the hell did you do that so fast?" I demand, still working the rope around my wrists. Ryan moves around so he's in front of me and meets my stunned expression. He reaches for my wrists and has them untied in less than ten seconds.

"I'm like Houdini when it comes to knots." He shrugs a shoulder and his brown eyes twinkle. Then he reaches out and closes my mouth, which I didn't even realize was hanging open.

My face flushes and his touch sears my skin, igniting a wave of desire low in my belly. *Oh, no, no, no.* I can't deal with this now. Shrugging off the loose ropes, I stand up and try to get my mind back on the problem at hand.

"We need to get Sierra," he says and heads for the door. "This is my fault."

I hate to admit it, but he's proving to be a reliable partner and maybe he's right. Maybe he might be able to help. As reluctant as I am to involve him, I decide to take him up on his offer. Backup is always a good thing to have and he's proving to be more competent than I could've imagined. Even though he told the bad guys where to find us.

"No, this way," I say and motion for him to follow me back to my room. "We don't have much time so we're taking a shortcut."

I tuck my backup gun in the waistband of my jeans and grab my backpack. After strapping it on, I grasp the cord and turn to Ryan. "C'mon. We're jumping."

Ryan's brown eyes widen, but he nods.

"Just wrap your arms around my waist and hang on tight," I instruct him, climbing over the edge of the balcony. Without any hesitation, he swings his long legs over the side and slides his arms around me. I pause. "You weigh less than 200 pounds, right?"

"One-eighty. Mostly muscle," he adds and my lips twitch.

"That works," I say and step off the edge. It's an easy jump, only three floors, and the wind whips my hair back as we sail down, the cord slowing our descent just enough the last ten feet so it seems as though we're floating down to the ground.

When our feet hit the grass, Ryan releases me and I undo the straps.

"That was fucking amazing," he says sounding more than a little giddy.

I can't hide my smile and a strange fluttering fills my stomach when I look up at him. "C'mon. They have to pass this way to leave." If my calculations are correct, we're one step ahead because we're already on the other side of the building while they have to make their way around and through the entire hotel.

"There," Ryan whispers and points to a perfect hiding spot. I follow him into a dark section of trees and bushes, right beside the path that the bad guys will need to take to get to the parking lot.

I suppose there's always the possibility they parked elsewhere, but I seriously doubt they valeted, and they'd want to be able to sneak away without a lot of people noticing. If it were me, I'd park my getaway car in the far corner of the lot out back. Guess we're about to find out.

Ryan hunches down beside me and our shoulders press together as we wait. "Do you have a boyfriend?" he asks in a low voice.

His question completely catches me off-guard. "What?"

"A significant other? Love of your life? Baby daddy?"

I don't know whether to laugh or tell him to shut the hell up. "No," I finally manage to say. When he doesn't comment further, I glance over at him and frown. "Why?"

"Just curious," he says.

I see a lot more than curiosity on his face and my gaze dips to his mouth. He has really nice lips and they look extremely kissable. Swallowing hard, I force my attention back to the pathway. "They should be here any minute."

"You have a plan?"

"Yeah."

"You gonna share it with me?"

"My plan is to get Sierra back by any means necessary."

"What do you want me to do?" he asks.

Stay out of the way. "Back me up," I tell him instead.

"Sure thing, boss," he says.

He's so damn serious and it's too cute. I press my lips together, trying not to smile. Ryan Mercer is proving to be unpredictable and surprising me in ways that I'm not really ready for. Normally, I can read a person and situation easily, but I'm learning there's much more to Binary Guy than meets the eye.

And I like it. A lot.

The sound of approaching footsteps on the gravel makes us both tense up. I lift my gun, ready to pounce and, a moment later, Sierra appears, flanked by the three mercs.

"I got the tall one on the left," Ryan murmurs at my ear.

Yeah, he's impressing the hell out of me. "Roger," I whisper back.

The moment they walk past our hiding spot, I nudge Ryan and we silently slip out. I knock out the shorter man with the butt of my pistol while Ryan slams a rock against the back of the taller guy's head. As they drop, the third merc spins and I drive my palm up hard, catching him right beneath the chin and snapping his head back. Then I finish him off with a roundhouse kick and he drops like a sack of potatoes.

"Oh, thank goodness!" Sierra exclaims.

"C'mon," I say. "We need to get out of here."

As we jog back up to our suite, Sierra starts gushing about how amazing we are for coming to her rescue. "I didn't know what to do so I lied about the combination being at the bank. I hope that was okay."

"You did good, Sierra," I say and glance over at Ryan. "You both did. But we need to grab our stuff and get out of here before they come back."

"Where are we going?" Sierra asks.

"A safehouse," I say.

"Oh, my gosh, I feel like I'm on an episode of S.W.A.T. Where's Shemar Moore?" she asks and fans herself.

I try to ignore the feeling that I'm babysitting and when we get to the suite, I tell Sierra to grab her stuff fast while I get mine. Meanwhile, Ryan reaches for his recently-returned roller case.

"You have two minutes!" I yell and race into my room. I throw everything into my suitcase and reach for my weapons case. The sooner we get out of here, the safer I'll feel.

In less than two minutes, we head out together. *What a strange, dysfunctional crew we are,* I think. It's almost comical.

"How are we getting to the safehouse?" Ryan asks.

"We're going to borrow someone's car," I say.

"Like steal it?"

I flash him my most innocent look. "They'll get it back. Eventually."

Ryan smiles at me and once again my stomach does a little dance. He's making me feel things I haven't felt in a very long time. Hell, ever. And with every moment that passes, I'm more attracted to him.

We manage to avoid the bad guys by following an employee pathway that leads directly out to Beverly Boulevard. Once we hit the palm tree-lined street, I study the various cars parked in the driveways of nearby residences.

"The BMW," I say and nod at the luxury car sitting in a driveway two doors down. I'm glad it's dark out and quickly scan the area for security cameras as we sneak up the driveway. The lights glow brightly in the house and it looks like the whole gang is home. That might deter someone else, but not me.

"Why this one?" Ryan asks quietly. "Blends in better? Faster?"

"Because BMW owners drive like assholes. Think they own the road."

He stifles a laugh as I reach into the side pocket of my backpack and pull out two small devices which resemble key fobs. I hand one to Ryan. "Stand right here and hold this."

Ryan takes the small, box-like device and I walk

closer to the house. Raising my device, I move it around slowly trying to pick up the signal from the key fob inside the house and transmit it to Ryan's device. It takes a moment and then I see the BMW's lights flash. *Click.* The car unlocks and immediately starts.

I jog back over. "Get in!"

Once we're all inside, Ryan and Sierra stare at me looking half-impressed, half-scared. I have that effect on people.

"How the hell did you do that?" Ryan asks and hands the box back to me.

"It's an RF device. You can steal keyless-start cars by picking up the radio signal from the key fob then transmitting it to the second device which will open the door and turn the car on."

"That's fantastic!" Sierra exclaims, moving up behind us and leaning over the seat.

"Fantastic and illegal," I say and head toward the safehouse in Burbank.

"I feel bad about this," Ryan says.

"About what?" Sierra asks.

"I guess my Good Samaritan was actually a bad

guy."

"It's not your fault," I say. "I should've caught on sooner."

"We're safe now and that's all that matters," Sierra announces.

Twenty-five minutes later, we reach the safehouse and I'm relieved to finally be somewhere where I can relax and have time to come up with a game plan.

After locating the hidden key, I open the door and we all trudge in, dragging our bags behind us. It's a decent-sized, ranch-style house with four bedrooms in a quiet neighborhood. I don't anticipate any trouble.

"Go ahead and pick a room," I say, pulling out my phone. I need to call Dash and explain the situation. Sierra heads down the hallway toward the master bedroom, but Ryan lingers.

"Hey, Fallon," Dash says, on speaker.

"Hi, Dash." While I give him the current SITREP, Ryan listens.

"I'm sending backup," Dash says. "Maddox can drive up tomorrow."

"Thanks. The fashion show is the day after tomorrow and we'll need to come up with security detail and a plan. I've got an idea brewing."

"I have no doubt." He hesitates then asks, "Are you okay? You sound a little off."

A dull throbbing reminds me I got shot and I glance down at my arm. "Fine," I say.

"No, you're not," Ryan snaps and I scowl at him.

"Yes, I am."

"She got shot," Ryan says, tattling on me.

"What?" Dash's voice thunders over the line. "Jesus, Fallon. Is that true?"

"Thanks a lot," I grumble and send Ryan a murderous look.

He walks over, eyeing my arm. "The bullet grazed her upper arm. I can clean it up."

"Ryan, I assume," Dash says.

"Yeah. Ryan Mercer."

"There's a First Aid kit under the bathroom sink. Do it right now before you get an infection, Pierce."

I sigh and try not to be annoyed because I know they're just looking out for my best interest. "You're not my Commander anymore, Slater," I remind him. "And you are not the boss of me, Mercer," I tell Ryan.

"I'll take care of her," Ryan assures Dash.

My gaze lifts to meet his and a small tingle erupts along my spine. I can't help but wonder what it would be like to have Ryan take care of me in other ways. Intimate ways. Striking the thought from my head, I tell Dash I'll call him tomorrow.

After disconnecting the call, Ryan nods to a chair. "Sit," he says. "I want to look at your arm. Be right back." As he walks away, my gaze dips to check out his ass clad in fitted, black pants. *It's just too good,* I think, and bite the inside of my lower lip.

When he returns, he's carrying the First Aid kit and a wet washcloth.

Gone is the unsure boy next door and I'm kind of liking this dominant side of him. I carefully peel my leather jacket off and try not to cringe as I lift the sleeve of my black t-shirt, but it's stuck to my skin. *Shit.*

Ryan's eyes narrow at the sticky blood and he pulls a pair of scissors out of the kit. "Hold still, boss," he murmurs, and I freeze when he pulls the collar of my shirt up and begins to cut it off me.

My heart thumps wildly and I swallow hard as he carefully snips the cotton material and peels it away from the messy wound. Even though I hold the shredded shirt over my breasts, keeping myself covered, I'm suddenly very glad that I wore my black satin bra instead of my sports bra today.

"It's no big deal. Just a nick," I say, trying to play it off.

Ryan bends down and takes a closer look. "A graze," he confirms. "But that doesn't mean you ignore it. I'm going to clean it and if you don't need stitches then I'll wrap it up."

"I'm not going to the hospital for stitches," I tartly inform him as he kneels beside me.

"I can do them myself," he states, cleaning the blood away.

"Oh, right," I say. "I forgot you went to medical school."

He pauses wiping around the wound and meets my gaze. "Yeah. As of a couple weeks ago, I am officially a med school dropout. To the complete disappointment of my father which I think I mentioned." His mouth curves up in a smirk.

I look down at my arm and remember him saying he didn't like the sight of anything gory. "I'm sorry. I can clean it-"

"No, I got you," he assures me. "It's the trauma and surgery aspect of it that always made me queasy. I thought I could get through it, but when a motorcycle crash victim came in three weeks ago, I knew I was done."

"Oh, God. That must've been horrible."

"I've never seen so many compound fractures in my life. It's a miracle he survived." Ryan pours some alcohol on a cloth. "This is going to sting."

I grimace and nod. It stings like hell and I grit my teeth. *You've been through much worse,* I remind myself.

"Okay?" he asks.

I force another nod. "This isn't my first war injury."

"I get the feeling you're a pro at this."

"I am. Ten years in the military and injuries kind

of come with the territory."

"Right. Delta Force," he says.

As Ryan begins to wrap gauze around my arm, I breathe in his clean, soapy smell and my stomach somersaults. I can't remember the last time a man had the butterflies effect on me. I was way too quick to judge him. Ryan Mercer is good under pressure, competent, fearless and kind. Those are all pretty important and vital qualities to possess for someone considering becoming a doctor. *But he's also adorable as hell*, I think, staring at his tousled brown hair as he secures the bandage and looks up.

Our gazes collide and electricity seems to crackle between us. It's potent and undeniable. Suddenly, our mouths crash together in a heated kiss. Ryan is still on his knees beside me and I lean down just a bit. He reaches up to cup my face with one hand while the other covers my leg, slowly sliding up my thigh.

His lips move over mine, coaxing them apart, and our tongues meet and glide against each other. *Holy hell, Binary Guy knows how to kiss a girl senseless.* My heart thumps as his hand pauses at the top of my thigh and lightly squeezes. *Mmmm.*

I'm on the verge of sliding off the chair and into

his arms when a phone rings.

Chapter Ten: Ryan

Pulling away from Fallon's soft mouth is the last thing I want to do, but my phone is ringing and killing the mood. I pull it out of my pocket and look down at the caller ID– unknown.

"I should probably get this," I say and she nods, looking a little dazed, clutching her shirt to her chest. Swiping the bar over, I say hello.

"Hi, is this Ryan?" a female voice asks.

"This is Ryan. Who's this?"

"Hi, it's Krista."

I'm still coming down from the most amazing

kiss I've ever had and my fuzzy brain takes a moment to process her words. *Krista. The Sure Thing. Shit.*

"Um, hi," I say and turn away from Fallon. Talk about shitty timing.

"I hope you don't mind me calling, but I hadn't heard from you and Joe told me to give you a call."

Thanks, Joe. Thanks a lot. Sometimes I want to murder that guy. "Yeah, um, now isn't exactly a good time."

"You still want to get together, right?" she asks, voice dropping to a sexy purr.

I turn back around and look at the stunning woman with flowing ebony hair and aquamarine eyes watching me closely. The only one I want to get together with around here is Fallon Pierce. "I don't think so. My plans changed."

"Oh," she says, sounding disappointed. "That's too bad. Well, maybe next time."

"Yeah, next time," I echo, eyes locked with Fallon's.

"Bye then."

I pull the phone away from my ear and toss it

aside. "Sorry about that," I say.

"Who was that?" Fallon asks.

Lying isn't something I do very well and I have a feeling Fallon would see right through me if I tried. "Krista, a friend of a friend."

"You have plans with her?"

"I was supposed to hook up with her," I admit.

My candidness catches her off-guard. "Oh. Sorry if I ruined your plans," she says in a dry voice.

There's no mistaking the jealous undertone and it boosts my confidence. "I'm glad you did."

Fallon arches a dark brow. "I'm sure."

"We've never even met," I tell her.

"But you had plans to sleep with her?"

I shrug. "My friend Joe set it up. He thought it had been too long since I..." *How to put this tactfully?* "...was with a woman. So he got this brilliant idea that I should take a much-needed vacation out here and get laid. Little did I know I'd run into you and all of my plans would change."

Fallon stands up and steps closer. "So, this Sure Thing…have you ever seen her?"

I shake my head. "Nope. And that conversation was the first time we ever spoke."

She seems to be considering my words. "You really came all the way out to California to get laid?"

"I mostly came for a break and to relax before starting up working again. Joe can be kind of an idiot."

"Well, I think you may have other options now," she murmurs, voice low and breathy.

"I do?"

Fallon nods, letting her shredded t-shirt fall off.

It's all the encouragement I need. I grab her, yank her against the length of my body and kiss her hard. When I want something, I don't hesitate and right now, I want Fallon. I want her with an all-consuming need and potent desire that pulses through every single nerve ending.

I've never claimed to be the best at anything but when it comes to my memory, I retain everything. Years and years of studying human anatomy have taught me some things about women's bodies and the best ways to pleasure them. And right now, I'm laser-focused and planning to take Fallon right to the edge.

Our mouths meld and I slide my leg between hers, reach around to cup her ass, and draw her closer, high up on my thigh. Fallon whimpers and all this damn denim has to go. I pull my lips away, breaking the kiss, and hear my own rapid heartbeat hammering in my ears. Fuck, she's got me so hard it's painful.

"Where's your room?" she asks, voice low and seductive.

I didn't pick one yet, but Sierra chose a room on the right side of the house, so I purposely go in the opposite direction. I grab Fallon's hand and guide her toward the hallway on the left, all the way down. I snag my suitcase as I pass it because if I'm very lucky, I'll be needing what's in there later.

The moment we reach the furthest room, I pull Fallon inside, kick the door shut and shove her back up against the wall, claiming her mouth in a long, hot, wet kiss. I know she's used to calling the shots, but I want her to know that I'm in control right now. I snake my fingers around her wrist and drag it over her head, locking it against the wall, careful not to touch her bandaged arm. She bucks against me once but submits when I grind my hips into hers, letting her feel exactly what she's doing to me. Showing her how much I want her.

Everything about her turns me on. I've never met a woman like her and I'm not about to fuck this up by acting like the tentative, unsure, submissive geek she probably expects. I'm not one to brag, but I know how to make a woman scream. And I want to make Fallon shout my name to the heavens above.

I release her wrist, spin her around and drop down on the bed with her, mindful of her arm. Her expression tells me I'm right– she didn't expect me to be so dominant and self-assured– and she likes it. I can see the sultry way her blue-green eyes light up.

Sliding back, I reach down, unbutton her jeans and pull the zipper down. When I hook my fingers in the sides and tug her black panties down with them, I can feel her tense up. My hand slides up, caressing her flat stomach, and I capture her mouth in a slow, sensuous way that has her arching beneath me.

When we finally come up for air, everything around us seems hazy and slightly unfocused. I'm burning up for this woman and I can't wait to please her in every way possible. Moving back, I drop down in front of her, hands sliding up her thighs, spreading them further apart. My lips and tongue trail hot kisses around her knee and glide to the soft flesh of her inside thigh. The moment I start dragging my lips higher, she clamps her legs together.

Surprised, I look up and she's completely frozen. She's propped on her elbows, head up, and those alluring blue-green eyes blink back at me.

"I don't do that," she says, voice so low that I have to strain to hear her. "It's too– close."

My fingers lightly squeeze her thigh. I haven't seen the indomitable Fallon look nervous before and it's damn endearing. "That's the point. So I can be as close to you as possible."

She shakes her head.

"You don't like giving up control, do you?"

"It's not about that."

"No?" I don't believe her. I think relinquishing complete control is something she wasn't built to do and it terrifies her. But I'm not going to push her. I want her to be comfortable and if she's not ready then it's fine. For now, anyway.

I'm not the only one around here who likes a good challenge.

Fallon shakes her head, in complete denial about needing to be in control, and scoots away from me. I slide back over her lithe body and kiss her slowly, drawing it out until she's running her hands through my hair and writhing beneath me. When she's relaxed again, I caress her hip and then dip my hand between her thighs, barely touching her. Just letting my fingers hover lightly over her center where heat and wetness radiate. I'm dying to dip my fingers between her folds and tease her but I don't want to make her skittish again.

"Okay?" I ask and start kissing her neck.

She releases a shaky breath, sinking further into the mattress. "Mm-hmm."

I part her slick, hot entrance and stroke until she's moaning, taking special attention with her taut clit, circling it and working her until she's panting and clawing at my back. By now most women would be in the throes of an orgasm, but Fallon holds out, making me use every trick I've got. "I'm not stopping until you come on my hand," I say and sink two fingers inside her. Her back arches and I move them in and out, trying to find that sweet spot.

A moment later, a cry slips out from between her lips and I can feel her body tighten and contract in a series of waves. *Bingo.* I pull back and admire the view– her dark head tilted back, eyes closed, lips parted and a rapturous look on her beautiful face.

And I love that I'm the one who did it. Even though I'm only starting to get to know her, I can pretty much guarantee one thing: Fallon normally holds back in bed. I want to break down every last wall of hers and expose every vulnerable corner because seeing her unravel is fucking magnificent. It's a huge turn on and my dick is dying to be inside her right now.

When her eyes finally flutter open, she catches me staring at her and flushes. "What?" she murmurs huskily, looking flustered.

"Watching you come was the best fucking thing I've ever seen," I growl. Before she can respond, I seize her mouth and kiss her hard. I swallow her moan and drag a hand up her side, covering her breast. *So full and perfect.* Even though she still has her bra on, I love how the soft, round globe fills my hand. I want to rip the satin barrier off, though, and taste her.

Rolling us slightly so I can reach behind her, I unclasp the hook and slide her bra off. My gaze dips, greedily admiring her rosy-tipped breasts. "God, you're perfect," I murmur and lean in to trace my tongue around a taut nipple.

Her hands slide through my hair and she arches, offering herself to me, and I latch on, sucking and licking. She's completely naked beneath me and I'm still fully dressed. Something about it is incredibly erotic.

But Fallon is getting impatient and she plucks at the buttons on my shirt, pulling them open. I help her and then shrug it off. Her eyes dip to check me out. I can see appreciation flash across her face, and the edge of my mouth lifts. *Good. I'm glad she's impressed.*

"Somebody works out," she says and runs a hand down my chest and over my ridged abs. When her fingers flick the button open on my pants and then tug the zipper down, I'm on the verge of blowing. "Nice palm trees."

I glance down at my boxer briefs and the palm trees are the last thing I'm thinking about when she tugs them down and my dick springs free. When her fingers wrap around me, I groan, dropping my head between my shoulders.

It's too damn good. And, yeah, Joe was right. It's been way too long. But I have a funny feeling that sex with Krista wouldn't have been anywhere near as exciting as it is with Fallon. I thrust my hips forward, filling her hand, breathing hard. "Christ, you're killing me," I grind out.

"You have a condom?"

"Yeah," I manage to say and pull back. I push off the bed, shuck my pants and boxer briefs all the way off, and go to rummage in my suitcase for the box of condoms that Joe gave me. I instantly regret calling him an idiot earlier and rip the box open.

Thank God for best friends who stick their nose in your business.

Chapter Eleven: Fallon

As Ryan digs through his suitcase, I watch the muscles flex in his tight glutes and my stomach drops in anticipation. When he turns back around, I still can't believe how cut he is. I mean, I could see he was in good shape but viewing him in all his naked glory is on a whole other level. I'm embarrassed when I realize I'm practically salivating for him.

He is as masculine as any guy I've ever dated, if not more so. Broad shoulders, firm pecs, washboard stomach and…my gaze drops to his big, straining cock. *Yeah. He's definitely not lacking in any way.*

I might be ready to have sex with him, but I'm definitely keeping my emotions locked down tight.

Right now is purely about the physical and I have no desire to take this past a one-night stand. We both need release and there's a mutual attraction so why the hell not?

Although, he's really prolonging the foreplay which I tend to limit or avoid. My bedroom experiences tend to be hard and fast. Hell, I don't think I was even in bed for the majority of my encounters. Not that there have been that many. Still though, I'm the Queen of the Quickie. That's how I prefer it. Keep things simple and straightforward. Getting emotionally involved isn't for me.

That's one of the reasons I don't like oral sex. It's too damn intimate and intimacy freaks me out. Guarding myself is important and my armor is thick. Life is cruel and I was a victim once.

But never again.

The mattress sags and, as Ryan rolls the protection on, my belly tightens and heat flares inside me. I don't think I've ever wanted anyone this much before and, as he positions himself between my legs, I lift my hips. *C'mon already!* I scream inside my head.

When he fists his cock and slowly drags it up and down my folds, I whimper. God, he's determined to prolong this torture and tease me until I'm begging. Desperate with need, I realize that I might have another orgasm before he even enters me. He lowers his mouth and starts kissing me and I'm so damn frustrated that I bite his lip. Maybe a little too hard.

He grunts and pulls back, eyeing me.

"Do it," I urge him. He's driving me insane.

"Are you ready?"

"God, yes!" I arch up and when he begins to push inside of me, I wrap my legs around his waist and try to draw him deeper. "I need all of you. *Now*."

As he slides in, nothing has ever felt so right. It's like my body was made to take him and we fit perfectly. He starts a slow, steady rhythm and I rock my hips with his, meeting each of his thrusts. The friction and heat build until we're moving faster, bodies slick, and I drop my head back as sensation pulls me somewhere I've never been before.

Ecstasy.

He slides his hand between our bodies and swirls that fucking magical finger around my clit until everything tenses and I feel like I'm going to break into a million wonderful pieces. *Oh, my Gooood.*

A cry bursts from my throat. Everything seems to shatter and my back arches up as a powerful release racks my entire body from head to toe. "*Fuuck...*" I cry, digging my nails into the hard, flexing muscles of his shoulders.

After one, two, three more powerful thrusts, he shudders above me. "*Christ,*" he hisses and then drops down beside me, ever mindful of my bandaged arm. We're both breathing hard and it feels like my heart is going to burst out of my chest. Whatever just happened between us isn't normal for me. Not even close.

I dare to look at him, trying to understand what I'm feeling. What he's feeling. His chocolate-brown gaze pours over me like warm Hershey's syrup, smooth and sweet. I'm at a loss and confusion fills me.

Ryan smooths a thumb over the crease between my brows. "You're not going to freak out on me, are you?" he asks.

How can he read me so easily? It's a little annoying. "I might," I say, deciding to go with the truth.

"Please, don't. That was fucking amazing, Fallon."

While that may be true, my mind is telling me to

get out of here now and go to my bedroom. I never linger after sex and I certainly don't spend the night cuddling afterward in someone else's bed. It's just not my style. Protecting others and myself is what I do and that includes my heart.

I roll away, grab a blanket off the end of the bed and wrap it around myself. After swiping up my jeans and underthings, I hesitate and Ryan sits up.

"Please, don't go," he says.

I chew on my inside lower lip and grasp the first excuse I can think of. "I'm working and need to be guarding Sierra." I know it sounds lame, but I don't care. Without another word, I walk out.

Ryan calls my name, but I ignore him. *I can't do this right now,* I think. Hurrying down the hallway, I step into the other bedroom, shut the door behind me and sink against it. A wave of panic, nearly as strong as the orgasm I just experienced, washes over me. I hate being vulnerable. It's the main reason I don't let myself get too involved with men. Serious relationships aren't for me and Ryan needs to understand that.

I drop my clothes on the chair and go into the bathroom to take a shower. The moment I lather up and inhale the sudsy soap, my thoughts return to Ryan and what we just did. *It was only sex. Why am I making such a big deal out of it?* I've always been able to walk away and not look back.

But Ryan Mercer is making me look back over my shoulder. He's making me wonder about all sorts of crazy things that I never do– like what it would be like to sleep in his arms all night and wake up beside him in the morning.

"Fuck," I hiss and slam the water off. I am so mad at myself for letting him get under my skin. I have enough on my plate right now guarding Sierra and the necklace. I don't need any more complications and I certainly don't need to fall for the magnetic man with the heart of gold in the other room.

No. Absolutely no fucking way, I tell myself and take a moment to mentally check that my walls are all still safely in place. After drying off, I slip my short nightshirt on and open the bathroom door. I stop short when I see Ryan sitting in the chair, waiting for me.

"What're you doing in here?" I ask.

"Can we talk?"

"There's nothing to talk about," I say and grab a bottle of detangling serum.

"I respectfully disagree," he insists.

Ugh. Leave it to Ryan to be so damn polite even in an argument. If I ignore him maybe he'll get the hint and go away. I turn to face the mirror, run the serum through the dark, wet strands of my hair and then begin to comb through it furiously.

"Fallon?"

My eyes meet his dark gaze in the mirror's reflection, but I remain quiet.

"I think you're really fucking amazing," he says and my traitorous hearts constricts.

I don't think he's going to give up easily and I hate to do this, but I'm going to have to be mean. Be mean to the man who's been so kind and attentive to me. *More than anyone else ever has*, a little voice reminds me.

But the words stick in my throat. I don't want to hurt his feelings. And I sure as hell don't want to set myself up to get hurt.

"When I came out here, I figured I'd hang at the beach, maybe take a drive up the coast. I never imagined meeting someone as exciting as you." The edge of his mouth lifts. "You're the best time I've ever had, Fallon."

Damn him. I slap the comb down and turn around, crossing my arms under my breasts. "I don't know what you want from me," I say.

"A chance," he says softly. "To see where things go."

"I can tell you exactly where things will go. After Sierra walks in the fashion show, I go back to San Diego and you go back to New York."

"It doesn't have to be that way."

"Yes, it does. I don't do relationships, especially not long distance ones."

"Fallon-"

"You're not hearing me. I had an itch, you scratched it, the end." I should stop, but I don't because I need to make it completely clear that whatever is going on between us is now officially over. "First of all, you're not even my type. We don't have anything in common and I think you're making a big deal out of nothing. What just happened is called a one-night stand, Ryan. That's it."

I see the hurt flash in his brown eyes and I hate

myself for putting it there. *You don't have a choice,* I remind myself. It's better to hurt him now than later. *Isn't it?*

Doubt fills me as he stands up, not even bothering to hide the devastated look on his face. Without another word, he turns on his heel and walks out.

"Shit," I whisper and tighten my arms around myself. I'm on the verge of running out and apologizing for being such an asshole but something holds me back. *Self-preservation.* Opening myself up to getting hurt isn't something I can do. It terrifies me.

I let out a shaky sigh and tears prick my eyes. At first, I just blink, confused at the wet sensation. I'd forgotten what it feels like to cry. I haven't cried since the day my parents died…and I survived. Because I should've died, too, right alongside them. The guilt still eats away at my soul and I don't think it will ever fully go away.

Ryan has no idea what he's asking of me and how hard true intimacy is for me. I can't explain my past to him and how it holds me back. He wants my complete trust and that's not something I can give him or anyone else. Other than Dash, Eden, Sailor and Maddox, of course. I trust them implicitly, with my very life.

Ryan needs a woman who will give him the very things that I can't. It's in both of our best interests to stop this before it goes any further. I know it's what needs to be done but...

God. The hurt look on his face kills me. Those brown eyes of his, so full of hope, reminded me of a dog at the pound who thinks you're going to adopt it. And then you don't. Seeing him deflate after I said he wasn't my type broke a piece of my heart off.

I've done a lot of hard things in my life but letting Ryan go may be the hardest.

"Shit," I whisper harshly. *I'm such a mess when it comes to my love life.* I turn the light off and fall into bed. My gun sits on the nightstand within reach, but I'm fairly positive that we're safe here.

"He's better off without you," I tell the darkness.

But my heart doesn't agree.

Chapter Twelve: Ryan

Back in my room, the hurt morphs into anger. Fallon prides herself on being so strong and such a badass, but she can't even confront her own feelings. She's so damn stubborn and refuses to acknowledge the connection between us.

Fine. If she wants to push me away, let her try. But I can be tenacious as hell when I believe in something. And, right now, I firmly believe that Fallon and I could have something really good if we can get past our hang-ups and doubts.

Of course, doubts plague me all night. I start second-guessing everything and wonder if maybe she really doesn't like me. Am I just a geek in her eyes?

Am I not someone she could see herself with? Was the sex not as good for her as it was for me?

When morning comes, I slip on jeans and a Star Wars t-shirt. I'm done trying to impress Fallon with overpriced clothes. I only have so much open to buy on my credit card and, let's face it, I am who I am. If she likes me then she likes all the different sides of me, too.

And if she doesn't…my chest tightens.

It's still early when I walk into the kitchen with my bag of coffee and supplies. I'm a coffee snob and travel with my caffeine goods like a true addict. As I'm setting up, Fallon walks in and I suck in a breath. Her hair is pulled back in a low ponytail and, as usual, she's dressed all in black. Those long, thick lashes snag my attention and when our gazes meet, she almost looks shy.

"Do you want some coffee?" I ask politely.

Fallon eyes my French press and measuring spoon. "What kind?" she asks and wanders closer.

"My own personal stash. Why?"

She steps up to the counter, gaze checking it out. "I'm just really particular about my coffee."

"Me, too." I hold up a ziplocked bag of ground beans. "How do you feel about arabica beans from Ethiopia? Particularly, the Harar region?"

"Oh, my God, are you serious?"

When a huge smile lights up her face, a part of me does a little dance inside. "I love the blueberry notes."

"Yes! They're so good." She eyes me. "I never pegged you for a coffee snob. I figured you liked Starbucks and-"

I slap a hand over my heart. "I'm beyond insulted."

We both laugh and it feels good to leave the tension from last night behind. At least for the moment. She hovers over my shoulder, watching as I carefully measure the ground coffee.

"Sorry it's already ground, but I figured it would be easier for the week if I didn't bring my grinder."

"Guess I'll let it slide," she murmurs.

I pour hot water into the French press and glance down at my watch to time the extraction. When I look up, I catch Fallon watching me closely. "What's up, boss?" I ask and smirk.

She shakes her head, looking a little flustered. "Nothing. You just...keep surprising me."

I lean a hip against the counter and cross my arms. "Really?" I drawl. "Hopefully in good ways."

"In very good ways," she murmurs, then moves over to the table and sits down.

She's purposely putting space between us and for someone so damn brave, I can feel the fear rolling off her. *But why would she be scared of me?* I wonder. I would never hurt her. With a sigh, I pour the coffee when it's ready and set the mug in front of her.

"Thank you," she says.

"You're welcome." I work on my cup while she blows on the hot caffeine and then braves a sip. "How's your arm?" I ask.

"Better."

"We should change the bandage," I say and she merely nods. "So what's the plan?"

"Maddox is coming up and we're going to figure that out."

"Is Maddox his first name?"

"Kane Maddox. He's a former Navy SEAL."

Of course, he is. I try to ignore the sour turn my gut takes and not think about all the alpha male badasses that she's worked with over the years. I can't help but wonder what the hell she sees in me. Well, I guess nothing since she wants to pretend last night never happened. Because let's face it, I'm no former SEAL or military hero with rippling muscles and a collection of guns.

I'm just me. Ryan Mercer, med school dropout who plays military video games.

I want to offer my help, but I know she's going to shake her head and probably stifle a laugh. Getting rejected after sex is bad enough for my ego. I don't need her reminding me that I'm just an ignorant civilian with no fighting skills.

Dammit. All I want to do is talk about last night and figure out why she's pushing me away but bringing it up now probably isn't a good idea. Fallon might be tough but she's also skittish. I figure the best thing I can do is give her space.

After watching her a moment too long, I tell her I'm going to sit outside.

"Not out front," she says.

"There's a back porch. With a couple of chairs," I add in case she wants to join me.

But, of course, she doesn't.

I have plenty of time to sit out here and feel sorry for myself because Sierra doesn't drag her butt out of bed for another couple of hours. At that point, I hear a deep voice and realize Kane Maddox must be here. Curious, I get up and wander back inside.

The former SEAL is everything I would've imagined and it's enough to give an everyday average Joe like me a complex. First of all, the man is huge and built like a damn mountain. He looks to be around 6'4" or taller and the circumference of his biceps is big enough to crush several throats at once.

Sierra stands beside Maddox, flirting up a storm, but he doesn't appear interested. In fact, he resembles a Rottweiler trying very hard to ignore the yappy chihuahua dancing around in front of it. His attention moves over to me when I step into the living room and I can tell he's sizing me up with a pair of alert, but cool, hazel eyes.

"Ryan, this is Kane Maddox," Fallon says.

When Kane offers his humongous, baseball mitt of a hand, I hope he doesn't try to show off his strength and crush my fingers. He takes it easy on my bones, though; his grip is firm but he's not trying to prove anything, and I appreciate that.

"Nice to meet you," I say.

"Likewise," he rumbles in a low, gritty voice. "I'm starving. Why don't we make some lunch and you guys can catch me up. I want to know everything that happened," Maddox says and Fallon flushes.

"Sure," she says, refusing to make eye contact with me.

Twenty minutes later, I'm eating a ham and cheese sandwich while Fallon finishes filling Maddox in on the men who broke into their suite at The Beverly Hills Hotel.

"They sound organized," he says, scarfing down a sandwich stacked high with every lunch meat available in the refrigerator. "Do you think it's a ring of organized thieves or lone wolves?"

"I'm not sure yet," Fallon says and picks at the crust on her bread. She looks over at Sierra who sips a Diet Coke. "Who else knows Armand gave you the necklace?"

"Well, technically, he didn't give it to me yet. I'm not supposed to open it until he's here for my birthday."

"Okay, so who else did you tell?"

"Well, you guys, my manager, a couple of my friends…" Her voice trails off and she claps a hand over her mouth.

"What?" Fallon asks.

"I may have posted a picture of the card on social media," she admits.

"Oh, fuck," Maddox grunts.

"But just the front of it. Obviously not the combination inside."

"Obviously," Fallon says in a dry voice.

"So the entire world knows," I say.

"Sorry. I'm just so used to posting every aspect of my life. It's so important to make your followers feel like they're part of your world and-"

"Sierra," I interrupt. "Did you post about being at The Beverly Hills Hotel?"

She nods. "Of course. That place is too gorg not to share."

Fallon and I exchange a look. "What about here?" I ask.

"This place isn't nearly as cool as the Bev," she assures us.

"But did you post anything at all?" Fallon asks, leaning forward.

"I mean, I shared a few things and took a photo of my room and the backyard," she admits. "Was that bad?"

"It isn't good," Fallon says and drags a hand over her face. A frustrated and very weary sigh escapes from between her lips. "You can't be logging in and posting on social media because hackers can trace us down through that."

"Sorry," she murmurs. "I didn't realize."

Fallon turns her attention to Maddox. "You think we need to move to a new place?"

"Possibly," he says. "Depends how smart these guys are that we're up against."

Sierra looks like she's about to burst into tears

and I lay a reassuring hand over hers. "Hey," I say, and she looks up. "It's okay. You didn't know." She gives me a grateful smile and nods.

I look over at Fallon who has a funny look on her face. But don't ask me what the hell it means. She's getting harder and harder to read.

"Where is this card?" Maddox asks.

Fallon pulls it out of her pocket and hands it to him. He studies the combination then closes it, setting it down on the table.

"We should get the necklace right now and head down to San Diego," he says.

"No! Tomorrow I'm walking in the most important show of my life. I can't miss it!" Sierra takes the card and begins shredding the corner of it between her fingers.

"My gut tells me they're going to strike at the fashion show," Fallon says. "Probably try to kidnap you in all the confusion and make you give them the combination. You're absolutely determined to walk in it?"

"Yes! Nothing is going to make me change my mind," she declares.

"Alright, then we need to make sure you stay safe. That's my number one priority. It's clear they want the combination and they know you have it. It's important that we keep control and always have the upper hand."

"How do we do that?" Sierra asks.

"By trading places," Fallon says. "A bait and switch."

"What?" I look over at Maddox who shrugs a huge shoulder.

"You two don't look anything alike," Maddox says.

"No shit, Maddox." Fallon rolls her eyes. "I'll need a blonde wig and if we do our makeup the same and switch clothing…"

"It will totally work!" Sierra exclaims, getting excited. "But I still don't understand. I want to walk the runway."

"You will," Fallon assures her. "After your final walk, we'll meet backstage, swap clothes and Maddox will spirit you out of there. While you two head straight down to San Diego, I'll lure the thieves in the opposite direction."

"I'll be your driver," I tell Fallon in a firm voice. For a moment, she looks on the verge of arguing but then relents.

"Okay, thank you," she says in that breathy voice and taps a slender finger on the table.

My gaze drops to Fallon's hand, remembering how her long, slim fingers felt as they trailed over my naked skin. My dick starts getting hard when I think about how her short, squared nails dug into my back and the hot, whimpering sounds she made right before she climaxed. I flex my shoulders and can feel the scratches she left there.

Damn. I shift in my seat, suddenly extremely hot and bothered. I'm never going to be able to forget last night and my breathing increases as I imagine spending another night with her. Fallon is a challenge and I want to tear down her walls, exposing every lovely inch of her.

I want to make her mine.

I'm ready to embrace every part of her, too. The good, the bad and the ugly. I just have to find a way to make it happen because Ms. Pierce is still an enigma on so many levels. I hate that she keeps shutting me down when I know we could be so damn good together.

My gaze travels up, moving away from her elegant hands and sliding up her bare arm to pause on her neck. Images of it arched back fill my head and I swallow hard, hands tightening into fists beneath the table. I look up and she's staring at me, an unreadable expression on her beautiful face. I want to jump across the table, pull her into my arms and kiss some sense into her.

Instead, we just lock gazes, slow blinking every once in a while, as Maddox asks Sierra some more questions that I only half hear. The energy between us is charged, heightened, and I can feel the need pulsing through me. I'm starving for her.

A throat clears and we both glance over at Maddox who looks from me to Fallon. His hazel eyes narrow then widen in amusement, but he refrains from commenting. I'm glad because I don't need Fallon pulling away even further if he starts teasing her.

"I think it'll work," Maddox says.

I'm actually surprised they're letting me take part in their plan. My role as the getaway driver for Fallon is important and while Maddox guards Sierra, I'll make sure Fallon is protected.

We spend the next hour going over every detail and then the girls go off in search of a blonde wig and other supplies so they can pull off the switch. I'm stuck hanging here with Maddox, and he pretty much keeps to himself. I'm surprised when he pulls out a book and disappears outside on the back porch to read. Who would've guessed the mountain man enjoys reading Moby Dick?

Hmm. Appearances can be deceiving. Hell, look at me. I'm a geek to the core, but Fallon sees past that. And Fallon, on the outside, projects toughness and strength. She wants everyone to believe she's so hard and unfeeling when deep down, I've seen just how fragile she is.

I'm tired and wander back to my room to rest. Hands behind my head, I think about Fallon and how the hell I'm going to make her see that she should give me a shot. *Give us a shot.*

Fallon and Sierra are gone for hours and when they finally return, they bring several large pizzas. We all sit at the kitchen table and devour every last slice. Even Sierra eats one. The girls tell us they have everything they need and we go over the plan for tomorrow again. I've noticed that Fallon and Maddox like to make plans for their plans. It must be a military thing.

After scarfing five slices of pepperoni pizza down, I take a long drink of water and my gaze dips to Fallon's bandaged arm. Maddox, who just devoured an entire pizza himself, must notice because he immediately asks how it is.

Fallon shrugs. "It's fine."

"I want to change your dressing," I remind her.

Maddox stands up, his chair scraping back along the floor. "It's getting late and I'm beat," he says and reaches down, his huge hands curving over Fallon's shoulders and squeezing. "Goddamn, you're tense, Dangerous." He squeezes them again and my eyes narrow. "Have the man give you a massage after he changes your bandage."

Fallon slaps Maddox away and he chuckles as he saunters off. Sierra hops up with a smirk and tells us she's going to get ready for bed, too.

"I need to do my nails, a face mask and meditate for a bit," she says and wanders away. "Tomorrow is a big day!"

"No social media!" Fallon calls after her.

"I know!"

After they disappear, I stand up and reach for the bandage on her arm. Very carefully, I unwrap it and take a moment to inspect the wound. "It looks good," I say. Grabbing the First Aid kit off the counter where we left it, I pull clean gauze and wrapping out. I hand her a couple of pain relievers which she pops without any water.

As I'm wrapping her arm, I can't help but wonder how close she and Maddox are. It's pretty clear they have a solid connection and seem to be on the same page. Jealousy flares up inside me when I think back on the way he so casually laid his hands on her shoulders. Like he'd done it a million times before.

She didn't even raise a brow.

"So, *Dangerous*…is that a term of endearment?"

"It's just a silly nickname."

"Do you have a nickname for him?"

"Yeah, his nickname is Idiot," she says.

"There's nothing going on between you two?"

Fallon glances up at me, a stunned look on her face. "Me and Maddox?" She bursts out laughing.

"God, no. Sailor would have a heart attack."

"Who's Sailor?"

"She works with us at Slater Security. Along with Eden. And Sailor has a massive crush on Maddox, though she'd rather die than admit it."

Some of the tension dissolves from my frame and I nod, finishing off securing the bandage.

"Why would you even think that?" she asks.

"He just…seems like the kind of man you'd be attracted to," I say and prop my hip against the counter.

"And what kind of man is that?" she asks, standing up, eyeing me closely.

"Oh, you know. The kind built like Thor."

Fallon hikes a dark brow up. "Do I detect a note of jealousy, Mercer?"

"A note? No," I say and stand up straight, arms dropping to my sides. "A whole goddamn symphony? Yeah."

Fuck. I shouldn't have said that but before I can regret it, Fallon places a hand on my chest, right over my heart, and I freeze.

"I don't want to like you, Ryan," she says, voice soft. Stormy aquamarine eyes lift to meet mine.

"Gee, thanks," I murmur and cover her hand with mine.

"I can't help it, though," she admits, and our fingers tangle.

"Why?" I ask, voice husky. "If I'm not your type...If I just scratched an itch..." My words trail off, reminding her of what she callously said.

"Oh, shut up," she says and slams her mouth against mine.

With a groan, we consume each other in a scorching kiss. Our tongues meet and clash and I can't get enough of her. God, I love how sweet she tastes and the way her body curves against mine. She possesses so much spice and a fire that'll burn me if I'm not careful.

Grabbing her thigh, I yank it up, wrapping it around me and press closer. I want her so badly, it hurts. When her hands run through my hair and she nips my bottom lip, I pull back, breathing hard. "You're giving me mixed messages, Fallon."

"I don't want any emotional entanglements," she says, wrapping her hand around my neck, grazing those nails across my skin. "Just a hard, fast fuck. Can you handle that?"

I slide my hands under her ass and jerk her up off the ground, wrapping her legs around my waist, and she gasps. "Can you?" I throw back at her.

"Don't you dare go falling in love with me, Ryan Mercer," she says.

My mouth edges up. "If you want casual and rough, I'm more than happy to oblige," I tell her.

I can see the excitement in her blue-green eyes and before she can change her mind, I head down to my room. *Back to the scene of the crime.* I'm not going to take it easy on her and I kick the door shut and toss her on the unmade bed. I'm still mad, but if she wants an alpha male, I'll fucking give her one. I pull my phone out of my pocket, pull up a rock playlist and crank the volume up. There are too many people around and they don't need to hear when we scream.

"Take your pants off," I say and reach for the button on my jeans. Kicking them off, I yank my shirt up and toss it on the floor. Fallon drops her black cargo pants and the edge of her mouth lifts as she eyes my boxers.

"Nice boxers."

They're the pair covered in trains. "Isn't it what's inside that counts?"

"Oh, yeah," she murmurs and reaches out, palming my straining dick and lightly squeezing. "How about your train takes a ride through my tunnel?" She attempts to slide her hand through the slit, but I pull back.

"Uh-uh." I grab her wrist and pull her up. When she's standing on the bed in front of me, I slide my hands under her t-shirt and around to her back, savoring the softness of her skin. She's beyond lovely but I know that's not what she wants to hear right now. So, instead, I rip her shirt up over her head and fling it aside.

My gaze slides down her perfect body, clad only in a midnight blue bra and matching panties, and my dick rises even higher and salutes in appreciation. *Thank you for your service.* When she reaches for me again, I step back, grab behind her calves and jerk. Fallon drops down on the mattress with a surprised gasp and I move over her, plundering her mouth with mine, thrusting my tongue against hers, and taking what I want.

She responds back with an enthusiasm that has me ready to blow. Whatever I did last night didn't work so time to change things up. *This time, she's not going to be able to walk away so easily.* I spin her around, pinning her wrists to the mattress and start kissing the back of her neck. When she tugs, trying to break free, I tighten my grip and hold her in place. "No. Don't move."

I'm going to make her submit to me– and not in the way she's expecting. *Emotionally.* Hopefully our combined heat will melt through her ice.

She's tense beneath me, but I don't let go. Just push her ebony hair aside and lick my way from her neck to the delicate dip between her shoulder blades. I feel the exact moment she melts. When she turns her face, cheek against the bedspread, and sinks into the mattress. Everything in her goes soft and a whisper of a sigh flutters from her mouth.

Good girl.

I nip her shoulder then finally let go of her wrists. Her hands clutch at the blanket and I begin kissing and licking my way down her spine. When I hear another soft sigh fill the air, I grab her hips and pull her up onto all fours. Fallon drops down on her elbows, breathing hard, and I drop kisses along her lower back, swirling my tongue above the cleft of her tight ass. Yet for being so firm, it's also damn soft and inviting. "Your ass is gorgeous," I murmur. "I want to fucking eat it."

A shudder runs through her and I bite a round cheek.

"Ryan!" When she tries to turn around, I tighten my hold on her hips then splay a hand against her back, making her go back down on her elbows.

"Hold still." Her thighs are too close together and I nudge a knee between them, forcing them further apart. She's digging her hands into the sheets but, for once, she's actually listening.

"Condom," she rasps.

"Not quite yet," I murmur and place a hot kiss directly between her legs on the narrow strip of her panties. Fallon refuses to let anyone get too close, telling me she doesn't let anyone go down on her, but she's letting me now. I use my tongue and teeth and it's not long before the thin silky scrap is soaked. Both from my mouth and her slick juices.

When I slide the material over, she tenses, and I

pause. I press a kiss against her hip and rest my cheek there. Waiting. Needing her permission. Wanting her submission. "Okay?"

It takes her a moment to answer, but she finally hisses out a yes. A smile curves my mouth, the rock song hits its crescendo and I drop my head, lifting her higher, and fucking go to town.

Fallon tastes just as sweet as I knew she would and knowing she placed a huge amount of trust in me makes my heart swell. Among other things. I work her panties out of my way, sliding them down her thighs, and reach around to find that little swollen nub. As I lick and stroke her with my tongue, my fingers massage until she's moaning and pushing back against my face.

Elation fills me. That incredible moment when Fallon lets go, gives up complete control, is the most beautiful thing in the world. I wasn't sure a woman as strong and stubborn as she is would ever be able to do it. But she's giving me everything right now, holding back nothing, and an array of emotions fills me– triumph, happiness, relief, ecstasy. But, most important of all, it's like she's giving me a gift– her complete trust– and I'm going to cherish the fuck out of it. As cheesy as it sounds, she's relinquishing her control, counting on me to safeguard her, and that's exactly what I'm going to do.

I'm going to take care of her in every way for as long as she lets me.

A moment later, she cries out and collapses forward. I lay down, half on top of her, propped on my elbow, and gently move her dark hair aside so I can press a kiss to her shoulder. A tremble runs through her and she's breathing hard. I lightly run a finger up and down her back and let her regroup.

I also need a minute to get my thudding heart and raging dick under control.

"I don't want any emotional entanglements. Just a hard, fast fuck. Can you handle that?"

"Can you?"

"Don't you dare go falling in love with me, Ryan Mercer."

A curse echoes through my head and I roll onto my back and stare up at the ceiling. *I'm emotionally involved.* No doubt about it. So much for trying to play the tough alpha when my heart feels like a fluffy, squishy marshmallow.

Fallon props herself up and turns to face me. "Guess I've been missing out," she says. "Or you're just really talented."

"I'm really talented," I say and she throws her head back and laughs. It's throaty, genuine and so damn attractive that I want to reach out and drag her onto my lap. Instead, I just admire her sparkling aquamarine eyes.

"We're not done here," she says and crawls over, straddling me.

I suck in a sharp breath as she slides my boxers down.

"Not even close," she murmurs and wraps her hands around my steel erection, slowly stroking. "You're mine, Mercer."

"Whatever you say, boss."

Yeah. I'm definitely at her mercy, ready to give her anything she wants. I grab her hips and dig my fingers into the firm flesh there, trying to maintain some semblance of control. She works me until I'm on the verge of losing my shit. Then she slides away and rummages around in my suitcase.

She's back on top of me in a heartbeat, tearing

the small packet open and slowly rolling the latex down my rock-hard dick. *Poor fella's ready to blow.* The moment she lifts herself over me, I'm done. I pull her down and thrust up, sliding deep.

We both groan and I sink back into the pillows and hand over the reins. Fallon splays her hands on my chest and tosses her dark hair back with a soft sigh. Her body begins to move in a slow, seductive rhythm, rocking back and forth, grinding against my pelvis and all I can do is watch. I am absolutely fucking mesmerized by her.

She's so fucking gorgeous and I lift my hips, following her lead. She still wears the sexy blue bra and I'm not sure what I did to get this lucky. She angles herself just right, finding friction where she needs it, and I enjoy the view, doing my damndest to hold out until she finds her pleasure first.

I reach down to help her along, toying with her clit until she's bucking. "Come for me, Fallon."

Her entire body tenses, tightening around me, and then falls forward. Our mouths connect, smothering her cry, and we kiss furiously. As the aftershock of her climax ripples through her, mine hits me like a fucking freight train. I groan long and hard into the soft curve of her neck, biting down on the tender flesh, as the hot pulse of release leaves me emptied and satiated.

"Holy shit," I whisper into her hair. Suddenly the music stops and all I hear is our combined, rapid breathing.

Chapter Thirteen: Fallon

My God! I can't believe how intense that was. I'm utterly spent. And now I'm lying on Ryan, trying to pull myself together, after experiencing the most powerful orgasm of my entire life. *Orgasms plural, actually.* I even let him go down on me. And I never do that. Relinquishing control isn't who I am. The fact that I just let my guard down with Ryan is a miracle.

While Ryan gets up to dispose of the condom, panic begins to creep in. He crawls back into bed a moment later and must sense it, because he tugs me against his firm chest, wrapping his arms around me. "Don't leave yet," he whispers. He places a soft kiss on my temple and I weaken instead of defaulting to my normal reaction to tense up and bolt.

"I don't cuddle," I remind him.

"Me neither." His arms tighten around me.

"Then what are we doing right now?"

"Relaxing." I can hear the smile in his voice.

It's late and I'm exhausted so I let myself lean into the curve of his body. *For just a little bit*, I tell myself. Then I'll leave and go back down to my room.

Then the strangest thing happens. For the first time in my life, I fall asleep with a man after sex. Unfortunately, I also dream and that usually means one thing. The nightmare returns and I'm 16 years old again. My parents and I are back in that goddamn gas station, and I have to face the incident that changed the course of my entire life. Again.

While my mom goes in search of a cold Diet Coke, the smell of hotdogs hits my nose. I wander over to peer through the glass at the dried-up links turning sadly on rotating metal spinners. They look like they've been in there for days and I can see why no one has bought them. Hmm, I decide to get a sandwich instead.

My parents and I are on our way home from visiting a friend's cottage up in Michigan for the past week. It was nice to swim in the lake and have cookouts, but I'm ready to get back home and see my friends. Seven days with my dad, mom and their friends in the middle of nowhere is enough for me. Adults aren't that fun and they proved it this past week when all they wanted to do was sit around the firepit, drink and reminisce about their time in college together. Boring.

I head over to the cooler and glance down at the sandwich choices. They don't look much better than the hotdogs and I frown. The bell over the front door dings and I glance over my shoulder to see my dad walk in and head to the counter to pay for the gas.

It's the second ding that I'll never forget. The moment when the man with the bandana covering his lower face walks in, waving a gun. I'm not really paying any attention until I hear a commotion and an edgy, muffled voice ordering my dad to back off.

I slowly turn and see the robber lift his gun, point it at the cashier and shoot. My mouth drops in shock as the man behind the counter flies backward and disappears from view. The moment the guy pulls the trigger, my dad launches forward and tackles the robber to the floor.

Time seems to stand still and the horrific roar of gunfire echoes through the small area again. My dad crumples and my mom comes racing around the corner. Her scream is worse than the sound of the gun going off.

Until it fires again and my mom staggers forward.

I'm frozen, unable to move, eyes filling with tears of disbelief. How did our lake trip turn into this? The sandwich drops from my hand, hits the floor and the robber looks over and makes eye contact with me. He has a glazed, wild-eyed look that makes me think he's high and he scrambles to his feet.

Outside, an SUV rolls up to the closest pump and the junkie seems to be weighing his options: shoot me, make a run for it or grab the cash from the register.

Greed wins out. He hops the counter and starts punching the keys on the cash register. When the drawer doesn't open right away, he slams an angry fist into it and curses. I'm still standing there, suspended in time, and my gaze lowers to my dad and the blood spilling across the linoleum floor. I can't see my mom fully. Just her legs, but it's clear that she's down and not moving.

A sob threatens to tear from my throat and I clap a hand over my mouth. When the door dings again, I see the SUV's owner walk in and abruptly stop. His eyes move from my parents to me to the robber in less than a second and then he's pulling a gun from a concealed holster beneath his light jacket.

It takes a moment for the drugged-up robber to realize we're not alone any longer and that the former military man who just walked in is now aiming a gun at him. The druggie, still unable to get the register open, is in an absolute rage, bandana now hanging down around his neck, not even trying to hide his identity anymore. Like some kind of feral animal with rabies, he's practically foaming at the mouth as he shouts a curse and grabs his weapon off the counter.

He's too slow, though, and the SUV owner, whose name I later find out is Sam, lifts his piece and fires a bullet right into the robber's heart. He drops, dying instantly, and falls on top of the cashier.

Something that sounds like a howl fills the air and I later realize it was me who made that horrible sound. I run over, standing between my fallen parents, and then drop down beside my mom. Horror of the worst kind hits me like a punch to the gut as I grab her arm and shake her.

"Mom, mom, mom…" I repeat the word over and over. Maybe if I say it enough, it will bring her back.

But, of course, it doesn't.

When the police and ambulance finally arrive, I'm covered in my parents' blood and numb with shock. And then the nightmare ends like it always does: I wake up screaming.

"Fallon! Wake up. You're okay."

My eyes snap open and someone is shaking my arm. *Where am I?* Confusion makes me lash out and shove the person away until a light flips on and the darkness falls away. When I see the concern in Ryan's dark eyes, I feel so stupid. I press the back of my hand over my mouth, stifling the sob that threatens. My entire body shakes and Ryan pulls me into his arms and squeezes hard.

"You're okay," he murmurs. "I've got you. You're safe."

For a moment too long, I allow myself to take comfort in his embrace and soft reassuring words. Then I pull away, not wanting to look like a weak fool. It's been a long time since I had the full dream from beginning to end. A lot of times it's only a snippet here or there, which is bad enough. But reliving the whole horrible event takes a toll on me.

I feel like I just experienced it all over again for

the first time and I can't stop shaking. Looking down, I can see their blood on me again and a sob tears from my throat. Tears roll down my face and I can't breathe. I slide out of bed and bend over at the waist, hands on my thighs, gasping for air. It's like I'm drowning, but it's agony filling my lungs rather than water.

I must be in the middle of a full-blown panic attack and I'm struggling to take a full, deep breath. But I can't. It's physically impossible because all I can see is my mom and dad, laying there in that gas station, dead. *So much blood.*

Hands move over my back, massaging up and down my spine and soft, soothing words are close to my ear. It takes me a second to realize Ryan is bent over with me, trying to calm me down. I'm focused on the floor, trying to get a damn grip, watching the silent tears fall from my lashes and disappear in the dark carpet fibers.

I've been through a lot of shit in my life and I pride myself on always keeping my cool. So the fact that I'm having a total meltdown in front of Ryan shocks me. My rapid breathing begins to slow down a bit. Finally, I find the strength to stand back up straight and cover my face with my hands.

"You're okay, baby. Just breathe."

I think it might be his soft, incessant chanting that finally calms me down. But that doesn't make it any less humiliating. I pinch the bridge of my nose and choke out an apology.

"There's nothing to be sorry for," he says softly. "We all have nightmares. I'm sure you've seen a lot."

As my cool control returns, I let out a breath, move away from him and swipe up my clothes. I start getting dressed fast because I have to get out of here. *Now*.

"Fallon, don't go. You're upset and-"

"I'm fine," I force out, pulling my shirt back on.

"No, you're not."

"Leave me alone, Ryan." I don't want his pity or to see the way he's looking at me. Like some sort of victim. It's bad enough that I have to live with the guilt of surviving, but I hate the sympathetic looks.

I can't find my stupid panties and I'm so frustrated that I just grab my cargo pants and pull them on.

"Fallon, please. Let me help."

I spin around and shake my head. "You can't.

There's nothing you can do except leave me alone. I'll work through it myself like I always do."

"But you don't have to," he insists and wraps a hand around my elbow. "You're not alone anymore."

"I don't-" My voice catches and I can feel myself getting upset again. No one has ever been there for me like this and it's freaking me the fuck out. "Let go," I say and yank my arm away.

"I know you want everyone to think you're this huge badass and you're not scared of anything," he says, brown eyes flashing. "But I see past that. Whatever it is, Fallon, I'll face it with you."

"It's too late," I say, sadness washing over me. Suddenly I'm so tired. Tired of pretending I don't still hurt, that the nightmares are over and that I'm stronger than I really am. I'm a broken, fucking mess despite what I work so hard to project to the world and Ryan deserves better.

"It's never too late," Ryan insists.

I shake my head. "The monster already won," I whisper and walk out.

Back in my room, I collapse on my bed. I just want to sink into the mattress and disappear. I work so hard at keeping my armor up and my true emotions well-concealed. I hate appearing vulnerable and I thought I'd come to terms with the tragedy that happened.

Apparently not.

Sleep eludes me for the rest of the night and thankfully Ryan leaves me to face my demons alone. At the first sign of light, I get up, take a shower and then sit on the bathroom counter with my makeup spread out beside me. I admire my new eyeshadow palette again and start applying my foundation. We have an important mission today, protecting Sierra and outsmarting some thieves, so that calls for a smokey eye. I think to apply makeup well you have to possess an artistic streak and steady hand. Luckily, I have both and, after the shitshow that happened last night, sitting here and spending a half an hour painting my face relaxes me.

After my makeup is perfection, I slick my hair back into a low bun, spritz my perfume on and get dressed. I carefully pack a small bag with the blonde wig, thigh holster, gun and a few other supplies. My pulse thrums and I'm ready for some action.

I delay leaving my bedroom until I can't any longer. We need to go over the plan one more time and make sure everyone is ready. I release a breath, step out into the hallway and head toward the kitchen where I can hear the others already talking.

"Morning," Maddox says when I appear. "Ready to do this?"

"Hell yeah," I say.

"Here you go," Ryan says and hands me a mug filled to the brim with his delicious Ethiopian coffee.

"Thanks," I say, avoiding eye contact. After last night, I can only imagine what he thinks about me now. *Probably that he dodged a bullet.* Yet I can't deny the thrill that runs through me when our fingers brush. I sit down at the table and focus on Sierra. "Ready?"

Sierra nods, more enthusiastic than I've ever seen her, and that's saying a lot. "Today is the biggest day of my life! Walking in this show is going to be the highlight of my career. So far," she adds with a dazzling smile.

"Don't forget. The moment you step off that stage-"

"I meet you, switch clothes and then duck out with Maddox. I know," she says.

I finally look over at Ryan. "And you're going to be in the alley-"

"Ready and waiting," he says.

"You think the thieves will make an appearance?" Maddox asks.

"I do. But, if they don't then no harm, no foul and we all go home." I glance over at Ryan and can't miss the momentary flash of disappointment on his face. "Either way, we got this handled."

Or, so I think, anyway.

The high-end fashion designer's show takes place in an airplane hangar at LAX. A bit unusual but when I walk inside, I'm blown away. It's been entirely transformed and resembles a desert oasis complete with a large stage and runway surrounded by sand, palm trees and even a big pool of water. The catwalk extends over the sand and beach chairs line it on either side. Cabanas and various tents are set up and serve tropical drinks with umbrellas. My eyes bug out of my head when I see a camel being led around. It's clear no expense was spared.

I'm hoping the bad guys come out to play. It's clear they want the necklace and I need something else to focus on other than my total meltdown last night.

My fingers tighten around the handles of the small bag I'm holding and I make my way over to the back corner of the stage, taking up position there. Then I touch the comms link in my ear. "Maddox? Ryan? Can you hear me?"

"Roger, Dangerous," Maddox instantly says.

"Ditto," Ryan replies and I smirk. His voice sounds good over the line and I feel a surge of confidence knowing both he and Maddox are here. I'm not super happy that Ryan is going to be more involved than I'd like and playing the role of getaway driver, but I have full confidence in him.

The hangar is packed with people and I even recognize a few celebrities in the front row facing the stage. When the lights finally go down and the music starts, I watch from my dark corner, alert gaze scanning over the crowd, looking for any suspicious characters.

The moment the models begin walking down the runway, cheers and applause erupt. Sierra Simone gets a ton of love from the crowd and it's clear she's in her element. She struts her stuff, long legs stomping, and at the end of the catwalk, she poses, turning this way and that.

"Uh, Dangerous?" Ryan says through my earpiece.

My mouth curves up. He really is too damn cute. "Go ahead, Mercer."

"A car with a couple of shady-looking dudes just rolled up outside the back door here."

"Shit. Did they see you?"

"Negative. I'm down, crouched out of view."

"Roger that. Stay down and keep me posted."

"Roger," he says.

I glance down at my watch and, right before Sierra makes her last sweep down the runway before the big finale, I slip around the edge of the stage and mix into the chaos currently happening behind the scenes. The director is lining the models up as they scramble to change into their final outfits, the designer is making last second adjustments and the air is pulsing with excited energy.

The booming music changes and the director yells, "Go, go!" to the first model in line. As they parade out one last time, I get into position behind a huge rack of clothes, kick my boots off, and wait. Two minutes later, Sierra hurries around the rack, pulling the gorgeous, one-of-a-kind scarlett evening gown off. I tug my cargo pants down and rip my t-shirt off, swapping clothes with her.

"I saw a man watching me and he looked really suspicious," she whisper-yells, yanking my pants up her slim hips. The music still plays loudly and the cacophony of excited voices and orders from the director echo around us.

Sliding the satin straps over my shoulders, I spin around. "Zip me up. Quick," I say and slip my feet back into my boots while strapping my gun and holster around my upper thigh. The dress is a few inches too long and I pull the long, blonde wig on, tucking my dark hair beneath it.

I adjust the dress then shove my bag into Sierra's hands as Maddox appears right on schedule.

"Possible tangoes," I warn him and he gives me a nod.

"Let's go," he says, placing a hand on Sierra's back and escorting her right into the crowd, toward the exit on the opposite side of the hangar.

Meanwhile, I touch my comms. "On my way out, Mercer. Any sign of the men you saw earlier?"

"No. They drove away. The coast is clear."

"Great. I should be there in-"

A large hand lands on my shoulder and yanks me around. I slam my hand down in a chop and his grip breaks.

"What the fuck?" the man snarls.

I hike the flowing, ruby red skirts up and launch a kick into his gut. *Glad I kept my boots on.* He doubles over with a grunt as I run for the back door. I can hear him chasing after me as I'm shoving through an endless crowd of people.

"Coming in hot with a tango on my tail!" I yell into my comms.

"Engine's running," Ryan says.

I blast out the back door, fist clutching the dress up above my knees, legs pumping hard and fast. Ryan has the car positioned just right, with the passenger side facing me, and he shoves the door open so I can dive inside. I'm barely in before he slams his foot down on the gas and we squeal up the alley, leaving a trail of black tire marks on the pavement.

I slam the door shut, pull my gun from the holster

buckled around my thigh and spin around to see if anyone is following us. "Fuck," I hiss when I spot a car peeling around the corner. "I hope you're ready to do some evasive driving."

Ryan glances in the rear view mirror and tightens his grip on the steering wheel. "Hang on," he says between gritted teeth and takes a sharp turn. My injured shoulder slams against the passenger side door and I stifle a groan.

Meanwhile a bullet strikes the back window.

Here we go.

Chapter Fourteen: Ryan

I yank the wheel hard to the left and I wouldn't be surprised if the car is jacked up on two wheels as we take the hairpin curve far too fast. Fallon rolls the window down and leans out. She squeezes off a couple of shots and spins back around.

"Stay right!" she shouts as we come up to a split to exit the airport. I hit the gas, cut two cars off, and we careen onto a side road.

We're in the Slater Security Range Rover that Maddox drove up from San Diego and the back window is already a huge spider web crack. I'm doing my best to lure these guys as far away as possible from Maddox and Sierra who should be driving in the opposite direction.

"Whoever these guys are, they want that combination really badly," I say. The moment the words are out of my mouth, they ram us from behind. Fallon flies forward and I shoot an arm out in front to protect her from hitting the dashboard.

"Thanks," she says. She glares over her shoulder. "At least we know the plan is working because they're coming after us."

My eyes are glued to the road but I toss her a quick smile. "You look good as a blonde," I tell her and weave the Rover through traffic, trying to shake the persistent assholes following us.

"I make a terrible blonde," she counters. "I'm not bubbly or sweet or flaky."

I chuckle as she fires another shot at the pursuing SUV. "True. You're definitely a brunette at heart."

She looks back inside at me and arches a dark brow. "Meaning?"

"You're saucy," I say.

Fallon bursts out laughing and aims at the other vehicle. *POP! POP!* This time, one of her shots makes contact with the front tire. The SUV jerks and spins out.

I pump a fist. "Yeah!" I exclaim and watch through the rear view mirror as they're forced to pull over to the side of the road. "Good shooting, boss."

She drops down in the seat with a triumphant grin. "Let's head back to Burbank."

Once we reach the safehouse, I shut the door behind us and turn to see Fallon staring at me with that look in her aquamarine eyes. "Have I told you how stunning you look in that dress?" My gaze dips, admiring the way the silky red gown falls over her curves. She clutches the blonde wig in her hand and I smirk. "It also looks much better on someone with dark hair."

Fallon throws herself against me and our mouths collide. Desire spikes between us, hot and fierce, so when a phone rings, it takes a moment for us to pull away from each other.

"That's me," she says and reaches into her bag. "Probably Maddox checking in. I'll be quick," she promises.

"I'm counting on it."

She looks down at the caller ID, sees his name and hits speaker. "Hey, Maddox, how's it going?"

"No, sorry, it's not Maddox."

Fallon and I exchange a shocked look and goosebumps raise on my arms.

"Who is this?" she demands.

"Maddox is currently unavailable and suffering from a pretty serious concussion right now," the low, gruff voice continues.

My heart drops into my shoes and Fallon's lips tighten into a thin line.

"You think you're so clever," the stranger continues. "But I've grown extremely tired of this cat and mouse bullshit."

Fallon's fingers tighten around the phone in a death-grip. "What do you want?"

"Same thing I've wanted since we met on the Santa Monica Pier. I want that fucking safe combination and if you don't give it to me now then I'm going to put a bullet in the big guy then the model."

"We don't have the card," Fallon says.

"That's interesting, but I'm going to share a little secret with you. I loathe liars. If you lie to me, I tend to pull the trigger rather than ask questions."

"We don't have it," Fallon insists. "I swear."

"That's funny because neither does she."

Fallon and I exchange a confused look. We both know Sierra has the card and, a moment later, her shaky voice comes over the line. "Fallon? I'm so sorry. I messed up."

"Are you and Maddox okay?" Fallon asks.

"They knocked him out," she says. "He still hasn't woken up yet."

"Listen to me, Sierra. I want you to give them the card. The necklace isn't worth your life." Fallon's voice is calm and controlled, but I can hear the underlying fear. We've lost the upper hand and not being in control is Fallon's worst nightmare.

"I can't," she says. "That's the problem. I was so sick of that stupid card and all the trouble it's caused so I-" her voice cuts off.

"You what?" Fallon asks.

"I destroyed it."

Oh, shitballs. Fallon's head drops back and I know exactly what she's thinking. That we have nothing left to bargain with. *That's not exactly true, though.*

"Who else has the combination?" the man barks.

"My boyfriend," Sierra says.

"I suggest you get it from him or I start shooting."

"He's out of the country until-"

"Enough with the excuses!" the thug yells. Sierra cries out and it sounds like he hit her.

Fuck. Time to step up and play hero. "I have it," I say.

"What?" Fallon and the man respond at the same time.

"That's right." Our gazes lock and I tap the side of my head, reminding her I remember everything that I see. Even a 20-digit long sequence that I quickly read in a birthday card a few nights ago.

"Where is it?" the man snaps.

"In my head," I say.

"Ryan, no!" Fallon says and grabs my arm.

"Don't fuck with me, kid," he snarls and I hear Sierra whimper.

"I'm not! I saw the combination and I have a photographic memory."

For a long moment, the man on the other end of the line doesn't say anything and Fallon's blue-green eyes stare at me, completely unreadable. I'm not sure if she thinks I'm brave or a complete idiot.

Finally, the man clears his throat and says, "Fine. Let's set up a dead drop."

"A dead drop?" Fallon repeats.

"That's right. You're going to leave Memory Guy where I tell you and when I'm sure the coast is clear, I'll have my men pick him up. But, if you try to pull a fast one, all three get a bullet in the forehead. Got it?"

"Got it," Fallon growls in a low voice.

"I'll send you the location soon. And, I swear, if you try to fuck with me, you will regret it."

The moment he disconnects, Fallon drops the phone. "What the hell are you thinking?"

"They're in trouble and I can give them the combination."

"They're not just going to let the three of you walk away after they get what they want. These are bad guys, Ryan, and-" Her voice cracks.

"I know, but I have to help. And, hey, you know I'm counting on you to rescue me."

I'm trying to lighten the mood, doing my damndest to coax a smile out of her, but Fallon is upset. "They're not going to get away with this," she says and grabs her phone. "I'm bringing in reinforcements."

"More Slater Security?"

She nods. "I need my girls."

Chapter Fifteen: Fallon

My girls, better known as Slater's very own Charlie's Angels, are livid when they hear what's happening. A flurry of creative expletives fill the line from Eden and Sailor is quiet for a long, scary moment.

"If they hurt Maddox, I will string them up by their stubby little cocks, cut their shriveled balls off and shove that shit down their throats," Sailor finally grits out.

I knew that was coming. Sailor doesn't even try to hide her worry for Maddox and I tell her that we'll get him back soon. "Don't worry," I add. "You know he can take care of himself."

"He's not as tough as everyone thinks," she murmurs.

"We will get them back," I assure her. "Now hurry up and get here."

After hanging up, they leave to hop on Slater Security's private jet. Luckily, it's a quick trip. Wheels up to wheels down on the runway is 26 minutes, and I feel much better knowing that my girls will be here soon.

However, I'm now worried about Ryan. I can't believe he voluntarily tangled himself up in this clusterfuck. He came out here with the intention of having a quiet, relaxing trip and getting laid by a Sure Thing with no strings attached.

Instead, he ends up caught in the middle of a shitstorm. Between dodging bullets and running from bad guys, I'm starting to feel really bad for him. Instead of happy-go-lucky Krista, he gets me with all my emotional baggage. *Poor Binary Guy.*

"You don't have to do this," I say and lay a hand on his arm. I know he isn't trained for this type of situation and maybe it's best if we three girls figure out a way to handle it ourselves.

"You can't change my mind so don't waste your

energy trying," he says. "I'm all in, boss."

My heart constricts. No one's ever been all in like Ryan Mercer. The man must be a saint because he tolerates my bullshit and keeps coming back for more. Or maybe he's just a masochist. "Are you sure?" I ask, still reluctant. "The girls and I-"

"I'm sure," he insists.

God, I love his loyalty. It's unwavering and true. *He'd be the best boyfriend in the world,* I think. I know I don't deserve him, but he's stirring up so many emotions that I've kept under wraps for far too long. Confusion fills me and I'm not sure what to do anymore. A part of me really wants to try to make things work with him.

"What're you thinking?" he asks and runs his hands up my arms, carefully avoiding my wound.

This is where I'd normally push him away and give a curt reply, but instead, I look up into his chocolate eyes and my stomach flips. "I'm thinking…" My voice falters and he pulls me closer, pressing his forehead against mine.

"Hmm?"

"How much I like you," I admit.

He pulls back, gaze searching mine, and I give him a little smile.

"I know this probably isn't the correct alpha, macho response, but do you know how happy that makes me?"

His mouth edges up and my gaze drops to the sexy stubble he's been sporting. I let out a soft sigh, feeling myself give in to him. "I have no idea what you see in me."

He chuckles. "I see everything. I see *you*. You have more sides than a myriagon and I love every one, Fallon."

I frown. "What's a myriagon?"

"A polygon with 10,000 sides."

I can't help but laugh. "You're such a geek."

"Your geek," he says without missing a beat.

I'm not going to lie. My heart kind of melts at that. "I don't know anything about polygons," I say, still trying to deflect. "I'm also grumpy, stubborn and hog the blankets."

"You're also loyal, strong and when you're in bed with me, you can do whatever you want, baby."

I can't help but smile. "Charmer."

"Is it working?"

"Yeah," I say slowly, but I'm not referring to his last comment. "Somehow I think it is working."

"Does that mean what I think it means?" Hope blazes bright in his brown eyes.

When I nod my head, he takes my face in his hands and brushes his lips over mine. The kiss deepens and I reach up, covering his hands with mine. Kissing Ryan is unlike anything else. There's something about the way we fit together so easily. Being with him is effortless.

"I'm going to protect you," I tell him.

"I'm going to protect you, too," he says.

If the situation weren't so dire, I'd be ready to head into Ryan's bedroom and not come out until morning. Now that I'm warming up to the idea of a possible relationship with him, I want to get to know more about him. "Fair warning," I say, running a hand through his hair. "Letting my guard down isn't going to be easy."

Ryan lifts a strand of my hair and rubs it between

his thumb and forefinger. "I have faith in you."

I pull his face down and kiss him in answer. As our tongues tangle and the hunger between us builds, the front door flies open and Eden and Sailor walk inside.

"Who the hell are you sucking face with?" Eden demands, placing a hand on her hip.

"Eden Esposito meet Ryan Mercer. And that's Sailor Shaw," I add and lean my cheek against his chest.

"Nice to meet you," he says.

I feel the deep rumble of his voice against my face and, even though I want to tighten my arms around him, I pull back. Eden and Sailor are gawking like we both have two heads.

"We have a lot of catching up to do," Eden says and drops her bag. "But first we need the current SITREP."

"Yeah," Sailor says. "Where the hell is Maddox?"

"Everything was going according to plan and the switch with Sierra at the fashion show went off without a hitch. We thought we had lured the bad guys away, but then we got a call when we got back here. He and Sierra were caught. Maddox was knocked out and it sounds like he may have a serious concussion."

"Those bastards," Sailor hisses.

I exchange a concerned look with Eden because our girl rarely swears. Only Maddox has the ability to coax those nasty words out of her gum-popping mouth.

"He'll be alright, Sai. We all know Maddox can take care of himself," Eden says.

Sailor frowns and crosses her arms. "No word on where they want to do the dead drop yet?"

I shake my head and look over at Ryan. "You're sure about this?"

"A million percent so stop asking me. I'm the only one who knows that combination and I'm going to do everything I can to help get Maddox and Sierra back."

"Don't worry," Eden says and sweeps her long, dark hair over a shoulder. "We won't let anything happen to you."

"What's it like having a photographic memory?"

Sailor asks.

Ryan thinks for a moment. "It's like having a picture in your mind that you can pull up months or even years later. And every detail is crystal clear."

"That's crazy," Sailor says. "So if you turned around right now, what details would you remember about me and Eden?"

Ryan looks over at me and when I nod, he slowly turns around. "Sailor Shaw, you're maybe 5'4" in heels. Your eyes are bright blue like the color of the sky and your hair is blonde, darker at the roots, and you have dark eyebrows."

Eden snickers. "Because she needs to color it."

Sailor rolls her eyes. "I embrace my roots. Keep going, Ryan. I'm not impressed yet."

"There's nothing impressive about it," he says. "I just close my eyes and can picture you exactly as you are. You're wearing black cargo pants with-" He takes a moment to count. "-five pockets on each side. You've got combat boots on, double-laced, and a dark gray t-shirt with a string unraveling on the bottom right corner. You're wearing a military-looking watch on your right wrist and your fingernails are painted pink. You have small silver earrings and a matching necklace on, no rings and your hair is in two braids close to your head. There's a beauty mark high on your left cheek. I also saw a tattoo on your inner wrist that looks like a set of initials, but I didn't get a close enough look."

"That's a lot to take in in ten seconds," Sailor says.

Ryan turns back around. "Did I miss anything?"

"Nothing you can see," she murmurs.

"I can see you're worried about Maddox," Ryan says.

I know he's right and we all look at Sailor.

"You know he was captured once before," she says, voice low. "It just…concerns me."

Eden and I know that Sailor is referring to his time in the SEALs when he was briefly captured by the Taliban. He doesn't talk about his time as a P.O.W. so no one knows any of the details. But I've seen him without his shirt on and the scars are disturbing.

"What about me?" Eden asks.

"You're kind of scary," Ryan says and Sailor and I chuckle.

When my phone rings, I swipe it up. "Hello?"

"I have the location for the dead drop," the man says. "Griffith Park. Drop the package off at the abandoned, old L.A. Zoo in exactly two hours. If I suspect anything, these two and Memory Guy die."

"And what happens after you get the combination?" I ask. "I want all three of them returned safely."

"Once I have the ruby necklace in my hands, your people will be dropped back off at Griffith Park."

"How can I trust you?"

"You don't have a choice."

He disconnects and I look at my girls. "What's the plan, ladies?" I ask. "Because I'm not thinking very clearly right now."

Ryan grabs my hand and squeezes.

"Well, there's no way in hell we can trust him," Eden says with a scoff and crosses her arms.

"Griffith Park. That place is huge," Ryan says.

"Lots of ways to sneak in and out," I add.

"I've been to the abandoned zoo," he says. "It was years ago but I doubt much has changed."

As Ryan fills us in on what to expect, Sailor opens her laptop and brings up images of old, iron cages covered in graffiti. "Super creepy," she says. "There are small cages, large animal exhibits, tunnels, locked gates. Lots of places to get trapped so be aware of your surroundings and avoid going inside the enclosures."

"Roger," I say and study Ryan. I know how much he wants to help, but I'm feeling so conflicted. My gut is telling me he's not ready for this.

"What's wrong?" he asks, squeezing my hand again.

"Have you ever taken self-defense?" He shakes his head. "I'd feel better about this if you knew some simple moves."

"Okay. Show me some stuff. I'm a quick learner."

"We can teach him a few things," Eden says and cracks her knuckles.

"Don't hurt him," I warn her. "I know how you get during sparring sessions."

"Me?" she asks, all innocently.

"Yeah, you. Remember when you broke Maddox's arm?"

"You broke King Kong's arm while sparring?" Ryan asks, suddenly looking alarmed.

"I'll go easy on you," Eden promises.

"Um, I don't know," he says.

"It's okay," I tell him. "I won't let her hurt you."

I'm not sure if my words give him any reassurance but I pull him over to the center of the room. Sailor pushes the coffee table out of the way and Eden rolls her neck from side to side. She loves to intimidate, but I let it slide.

"First, always trust your instincts," I say.

"Yeah. If the situation feels bad then most likely things are about to go FUBAR," Sailor says and snaps her gum.

"If you have the opportunity to escape, take it. No one is trying to be a hero and we all just want to stay alive at the end of the day."

"Confidence is key," Eden adds. "Keep your

head up, shoulders back and don't appear afraid, even if you're shitting your pants."

"The element of surprise combined with basic martial arts techniques will increase your chance of landing a blow first. C'mere." I tug him closer and lift my hand to demonstrate. "This is a palm heel strike."

With an open hand, I move my palm in slow motion and stop right before making contact under his chin.

"It'll snap your opponent's head back and, by keeping your hand open, you're less likely to hurt yourself."

"Got it," he says and runs through the move a few times.

I place my arms on Ryan's shoulders and drive my knee up, stopping right before I hit him. "A knee strike to the groin will end things real fast."

Eden and Sailor both release an evil chuckle. "I once asked Maddox what it feels like when a guy gets hit there and you know what he said?" Sailor asks. "It's like combining a muscle spasm, hitting your funny bone and breaking a bone all at once with a touch of vertigo and a hint of electrocution."

"That's pretty specific," Eden comments.

"And accurate," Ryan says and drops a protective hand over the front of his jeans. "Your stomach and chest tighten up so it feels like you can't breathe. That's why we fall down and curl up into the fetal position."

Eden waves a dismissive hand through the air. "Men are also big fucking babies so there's that, too."

"I'm sure it hurts but women have actual babies and I'm thinking childbirth is worse pain," Sailor says.

"The point is," I say, trying to get everybody back on track, "the fight isn't over until the threat no longer exists. You must be 110-percent committed to the battle. If you fight back and then pause, you give up the initial advantage you gained from using the element of surprise. Got it?"

Ryan nods and I take a step back and exchange a look with Eden and Sailor. "Okay. Let's practice in slow motion. Ready?"

"Wait. All of you at once?" he asks, suddenly uncomfortable.

"You look scared," Eden says.

"I don't think he can handle all three of us," Sailor adds, popping her gum.

Ryan's dark eyes narrow. "Bring it."

The girls smirk and we all move at once.

Yeah, poor Ryan is definitely not prepared for us, but Dangerous, Loco and Deadly are in the house and he needs to learn how to defend himself.

Chapter Sixteen: Ryan

Even though I know they're taking it easy on me, holy shit these women are fast, smooth and impressive. Their combined assault leaves me spinning, trying hard to keep up, but it's impossible. And we're still only moving in slow motion.

Fallon holds up a hand and Eden and Sailor fall back. They show me a few more strikes and a couple different ways to block. After practicing for a few minutes, Fallon tells me we're going to try it again, but faster this time. The women circle me, closing in, and my adrenaline kicks up. Even though I know it's not a real fight, I still feel like I'm the prey and they're about to take me down and devour me whole.

I raise my hands to block my face and turn

slowly, trying to keep an eye on all three. But the moment I blink, they charge. Eden chops, Sailor kicks and Fallon swings. And the entire time, they're moving back and forth with such grace that it resembles some kind of elegant dance.

When Eden comes in with a knee aimed at my groin, I jump back and block her with my forearm. I don't mean to hit quite so hard or fast. "Sorry," I quickly apologize.

Instead of being upset, she nods her approval. "Don't be sorry. Keep doing it. A solid block is the best way to let someone know their intrusion isn't welcome in your space."

I glance over at Fallon and she looks proud.

"You catch on fast," Fallon says.

"I have three good teachers."

Sailor nudges Fallon's elbow. "You already called dibs on him, right?"

Fallon's aquamarine eyes lock on mine. "Yes," she states. "So keep your hands to yourself, Shaw."

Her words make me feel like the King of the World. I don't think I've ever flown this high before and a big smile curves my mouth.

"Oh, alright," Sailor relents with a sigh.

"Besides, we're going to get your man back very soon."

"Kane Maddox is not my man," she says stubbornly.

"Hmm. We'll see." Eden tosses her a doubtful look.

"There's nothing to see. I mean, I'm worried. But only because he's my friend. My *work* friend."

"Whatever you say." Eden glances down at her watch. "How long does it take to get to this abandoned zoo?"

We decide to leave early and scope out the site of the dead drop. Griffith Park is huge and made up of over 4,200 acres of parkland, picnic areas and wilderness. The moment Eden drives us inside, there's the feeling of leaving the city behind and being swallowed up in the rugged terrain. We pass a lot of signs that warn hikers to watch out for rattlesnakes and mountain lions.

"Rattlesnakes and mountain lions?" Sailor

shivers. "Oh my."

"Just stay on the path," I tell them.

Beside me in the back seat, Fallon checks her gun then tucks it in her waistband beneath her leather jacket.

"Park by the carousel," I say and point to a large lot. "There's a dirt road up there behind it that leads to the old zoo."

"Do you *ever* forget anything?" Sailor asks.

I tilt my head and think for a moment. "No."

"Some days I think I'd forget my head if it wasn't attached."

"That's because you're a ditz, Sai," Eden says and pulls the Range Rover into a spot.

She shrugs a shoulder, not offended in the least. "Sometimes."

Fallon turns to face me, worry lines bracketing her mouth. "You're sure about this?"

"I'll be fine."

Eden and Sailor quietly slip out of the front and

give us some privacy.

Fallon lifts a hand and cups my face. "I'm going to get you back."

"I know," I tell her. "I'm not worried, boss."

She lets out a shaky breath and I trace a finger over her lower lip. Our heads lean in and we share a fast, hard kiss. "The tracker is secure?"

I flip my foot over and we both check the heel of my boot where she hid the small device. "All set."

"Okay," she says. "Please, be careful."

"You, too."

We get out of the SUV and start up the dirt road. It's about a 5-minute hike until we come to the top of the hill where a tall, chain link fence stands. "This is the back side of the big exhibits," I say and we all stop.

Fallon walks over and glances down. "I'm going to perch on top, right there," she says and points. "Eden, take the tunnel that leads down to the exhibit."

"Roger," she says.

"I'll be over there." Sailor points through the fence to the smaller animal cages. "When they come up the bend, I can alert you."

"Sounds good." Fallon touches her earpiece. "Comms check."

"Clear," Eden replies.

"Cry-stal," Sailor says with a snap of her gum.

"Alright, ladies. Let's do this so we can get my man back." Fallon turns to me. "Remember, you have the upper hand. You're the only one with the code. Don't give it to them until you're in front of that safe in Bel Air. Okay?"

She chews her lower lip and I hate seeing my former Delta Force badass look so edgy. "Roger that." My lips press quickly against hers. "I got this."

"We'll be close behind," she promises.

"I know." After squeezing her hands one more time, I head up the path further, circle around the exhibits and start walking down to the front. It's almost time and if the situation weren't so dire, it would almost be comical. When has a live person ever been the object of a dead drop?

Yet here I am– the dead drop of this operation.

Who knew a week ago I'd be in such a crazy

situation? I've got a combination in my head that will open a safe to a priceless ruby necklace. I'm head over heels for a gorgeous and exciting woman who I'd risk my heart and life for. And, now, I'm on the verge of potentially losing it all if this doesn't play out right.

It has to work. As long as I follow the plan, everything will fall into place. That's what I'm hoping, anyway, as I step into the large animal exhibit that at one time must've housed lions or tigers. *Or bears, oh, my!* I look up at the fake rock formations and notice that no one else is around. Normally, people sit at the picnic tables nearby or wander through the large enclosures and explore.

The place is eerily empty and I look up to where Fallon is perched. I don't see her and a wave of unease hits me hard. Suddenly, two men enter the area and head straight for me. The bigger guy motions for me. "Let's go."

My heart slams against my rib cage as I follow the two thugs down the dirt path and across the lawn. They lead me to an SUV with tinted windows parked along the side of the road.

"Get in," the shorter one grumbles.

Slipping into the backseat, I hope to God the

tracker in my boot is working so Fallon and her girls can follow us without any issues.

"Where are we headed, fellas? Bel Air?"

"Shut up," the driver snaps.

"Is that where you've got Sierra and Maddox?"

"I said shut the hell up!"

Bel Air is exactly where we're headed. Once we reach our destination, a large, ornate gate swings open and the SUV heads up a long driveway. Looking out the window, I gaze out over manicured lawns, flower beds, stone fountains and finally the house comes into view. Mansion is a better word to describe the enormous home. It's like one of those places that would've been featured on "Lifestyles of the Rich and Famous" or MTV's "Cribs."

Knowing how ridiculously overpriced real estate is in Southern California, I can only begin to imagine how much a place like this would go for. At least a cool $25 mil. Most likely more. I know we're in the neighborhood of "The One." I saw a special about the 105,000 square foot megamansion which sits on a leveled mountain. For a mere $295 million, the owner can have 21 bedrooms, 42 bathrooms, a nightclub, full-service beauty salon, spa, bowling alley, 30-car garage and a massive moat that surrounds the property.

Unless you're a multi-billionaire, it'll never happen. Luckily, I have zero interest in ever living in a mansion much less a mega one. But then I remember that Sierra is dating the Prince of Andorra and I'm about to help these crooks open a safe with a $5 million ruby necklace inside it.

I really hope Slater's Finest is close behind because my nerves kick up a notch. The car stops and I wipe my sweaty palms on my jeans.

"Out," the man in front barks.

Not wanting any trouble, I open the door, slide out and follow them into the huge house. We walk down a long hallway and reach an open door. The taller thug shoves me into the room and I key in on the man sitting at the large walnut desk.

"What took so long?" he asks and stands up.

"Traffic," the shorter man answers.

The man behind the desk moves around its edge and his dark, beady eyes seem to be sizing me up. Looking for a weakness. I just hope he doesn't see one in me. He reminds me of a weasel with his long neck, tubelike body and small, flattened head. I also get the impression he's just as clever and sneaky as the carnivorous predator.

"So, Mr. Memory, you still got that combination up in your pretty little head?"

"No," I say. Fallon would be so pissed at me right now, but I'm not about to give this asshole what he wants so he can turn around and shoot me.

He lifts a finger beside his ear and frowns like he didn't hear me right. "I'm sorry. What did you say?"

"Where are Sierra and Maddox? You need to let them go first."

"Let's get one thing clear. You're not the one calling the shots here, punk. I am."

I cross my arms. "Cool. But I'm the punk who can open the safe." The weasel's face turns bright red and I might've just crossed a line. *May as well go for broke.* "So unless you suddenly come up with the combination," I continue, "it's in your best interest to do what *I* say."

"Who the fuck is this kid?" he asks his men. When he walks over and stops right in front of me, I don't back down. Even though it's intimidating as hell. "You don't wanna give me the combo, fine. We can do this the hard way."

I grit my teeth, expecting him to pull out a gun. Instead, I feel a sharp prick in my neck and realize the taller thug just stabbed me with a syringe.

Oh, fuck. Fallon is going to kill me.

Chapter Seventeen: Fallon

It's no surprise that Ryan's tracker leads us straight to Prince Armand's house in Bel Air. The place is huge and pretentious. Definitely a place where royalty would kick back and hide behind their massive wrought-iron gates.

No gate can stop us, though. After Sailor jams the camera feed, we scale the 10-foot barrier with ease. Creeping forward together, we make our way to the side of the house and Eden uses a small tool to open the nearest window. The CIA taught her some handy tricks while she was active. But they messed up, lost her loyalty, and now we benefit from her training.

We slip inside what is clearly the library. Endless

books fill floor to ceiling shelves and several overstuffed chairs that would be great to curl up in and read look like no one has ever sat in them. I'll never understand rich people. They buy everything and rarely use any of it.

There's no need to say anything because we already know the plan and the three of us work together like a well–oiled machine. I give them a hand signal to hold their position and then walk over to the door so I can listen. It's quiet, but the house is huge. Sierra, Maddox and Ryan could be anywhere, together or all separate. The plan is to divide and conquer.

The coast is clear and I motion for my girls. We all have our guns in hand and won't hesitate to pull the trigger. I nod and we move into the hall in single formation, backs pressed to the wall. Once we establish it's safe, I move left and Eden and Sailor head right to find the staircase.

It's my job to sweep the ground floor and I move down the hallway on stealthy feet, clearing each room as I pass. So far, it's very quiet. *Suspiciously quiet*, I think, and pause near the corner. I hope to God they're okay. Ryan is a civilian and I never should've let him get involved. If something happens to him, I will never forgive myself.

Gritting my teeth together, I realize it's a mistake to underestimate him. He's smart, resourceful and has proven himself to be more than capable when the shit hits the fan. I'm so proud of him for stepping up and putting himself out there as bait.

I'm also terrified that he's going to get hurt.

Hang in there, Mercer. I'm coming.

After turning the corner, I start forward and hear the muted sound of a deep voice. It's coming from several doors ahead, and I sprint forward, stopping just outside the door, and listen.

"Go ahead. Keep playing games then. Eventually, you'll give up the combination."

I recognize the voice as the man who called me on my cell phone. *Is Ryan in there?* I wonder, and lean closer.

"Yeah, not gonna happen," Ryan says.

His voice sounds funny. Almost slurred and I frown.

"Do you guys have any idea how much trouble you're in?" Ryan asks. "My girl is gonna kick your asses and you'll regret ever tangling with us."

His girl? My heart constricts. *Yeah, I'm his motherfucking girl,* I think, and kick the door open. Three Rugers turn in my direction, but I'm already firing off a shot and rolling across the floor. The short thug goes down with a surprised shout. Their return fire misses and I yell out a warning to Ryan, telling him to get down.

Using a chair for cover, I pop around the side and shoot the second guy in the leg. He falls and the last man is hiding behind the desk. Suddenly, he stands up, yanking Ryan in front of him as a shield.

My gut coils when he places the gun's steel muzzle against Ryan's temple.

"Fallon, I'm assuming," the man says. His beady eyes and wide, flat forehead give me the creeps. "Tell your boyfriend here to give me the combination or I'll blow his fucking head off."

My gaze connects with Ryan's dark eyes and there's no way in hell I can take this asshole out without him shooting Ryan. "Don't hurt him," I say and slowly lift my hands, surrendering.

"Toss it," the thug says and nods to my Glock.

Without a choice, I throw the gun aside and raise my hands into the air again. Hopefully Eden or Sailor comes charging in, but I know they're busy scouring the rooms upstairs. If Ryan and I are getting out of this situation alive, it's because we're going to work together and outsmart this idiot.

"Don't move," he tells me then shoves Ryan over to the large safe set in the wall. "Punch that combo in now or the back of your head is going to be Jell-O."

I flinch when he pushes the gun into the base of Ryan's neck. When Ryan looks over at me, I nod.

"Don't look at her," he snarls. "Open the goddamn safe!"

"Okay! Geez." Ryan lifts a hand to the pad and hesitates. He pulls it back and rubs a finger against his temple.

"C'mon! What's the problem?"

"Whatever you gave me is making my brain fuzzy," Ryan says.

"What did you give him?" I ask, stomach sinking.

"You said you have a photographic memory!" the man yells.

"I do! Gimme a sec."

"We injected him with a truth serum," the thug tells me. "So if that combination is really up in your head, you better pull it out right now." He lowers the gun, pushing it hard between Ryan's shoulder blades.

Ryan's index finger hovers over the pad, but he doesn't punch any numbers in.

"You have exactly three seconds," the man growls. "Three…two…"

Ryan starts to punch in the string of numbers, letters and symbols.

I'm waiting with baited breath as he carefully punches in the random 20 characters. A moment later, the safe's door springs open and the thug makes a triumphant sound.

"Outta my way," he says and shoves Ryan.

The moment Ryan moves sideways, he brings his open palm down and slams it into the man's groin. *That's my man.* As the thug howls, I leap forward and snag my Glock off the couch where I tossed it. Meanwhile, the thug drops, hands over his crotch, and it looks like he has tears in his eyes.

"Don't move," I say and aim the gun. "Good job, Mercer. That was quite the hit."

"I remembered our training," he says with an adorable grin.

"You remember everything."

"Damn straight," he says.

I hear feet running and glance over to see Eden appear in the doorway. She holds up a few zip ties. "Need any?"

"Yes. For the three assholes on the floor." They're all groaning now and the sooner we restrain them the better.

After we bind the thieves' wrists, Eden tells me Sailor is with Maddox and Sierra. "They're both fine," she assures us. "We nabbed two tangoes, though, and they've been secured."

"Thanks, Eden." I turn to Ryan. "How're you feeling? They gave him some kind of truth serum."

He gives me another smile that makes my heart speed up. "Pretty good."

"I hate that fucking stuff," Eden says. "Makes you feel loopy for a few hours. But it'll wear off."

"Does it really work?" I ask and frown. Physically, Ryan appears fine, but he does seem a little off. Like he's had a few too many drinks.

Suddenly, he bursts out laughing at absolutely nothing.

"Better get him to drink some water and sit down for a minute. Sierra is talking to Armand and they just called the police. I'll get these douchebags out and lined up for the cops."

"Thanks." I walk over to Ryan and touch his arm. "Hey. You sure you're okay?"

"Smashing," he says. "Isn't that a great word? Makes me want to be British."

"I think you should sit down." I guide him over to the couch and, as we sit, he pulls me onto his lap.

"Ryan-"

"You just totally rescued me like the badass babe that you are."

"You looked like you had it under control. But I'm not going to lie. I was scared."

"Fallon Pierce was scared? Inconceivable."

"It's true." I grasp his face in my hands and then kiss him hard. All the pent-up worry drains out of me as our mouths meld. When we finally pull apart, I trace my fingers over his stubbled jawline. "I like the scruff."

"Do you find it smashing?" he teases.

I playfully push his face away. "You're crazy. You know that?"

"Crazy for you."

My heart kicks up a notch. "You're not thinking clearly. We need to get you some water."

He wraps his long fingers around my wrist. "Looking at you right now, I've never had more clarity. Don't freak out, but you need to know I'm not walking away from this. From us."

"You live in New York," I whisper.

"I could live on the moon and it wouldn't matter. Wherever you are is where I belong."

God. I want to believe his words so badly. "How can you be so sure?" I ask.

"Because I'm falling in love with you."

I suck in a sharp breath. "Ryan-"

He presses a finger against my lips. "No. Don't say anything. Not yet."

It's probably for the best because I don't know what the hell to say. Hearing him say the "L" word fills me with so many emotions. I manage a nod and he pulls his finger away. "I think I need a drink," I murmur.

Ryan laughs and sets me on my feet. "Hang on. I want to see this necklace everyone wants so badly."

Oh, right. I'd completely forgotten about the stupid thing. We walk over to the open safe and he reaches inside and removes a large black box.

"Go ahead," he says, giving me the honor.

I flip the lid open to reveal a glittering ruby surrounded by diamonds sitting on a bed of velvet. My mouth drops at the exquisite piece which is the size of a large strawberry. "Cupid's Bow. Wow. I guess I can see why they were after it."

"It's not nearly as smashing as you," he says and closes the lid.

I chuckle, slip my arm through his and guide him out. "Let's get you some water."

"Sure thing, boss."

Chapter Eighteen: Ryan

After drinking a bottle of water, I sit down while the Slater team handles the police. I'm finally starting to feel more like myself again. Sierra stares at the ruby necklace in her hands then finally looks over at me and says, "I think I have to break up with him."

"With your prince?"

She nods.

"How come?"

With a soft sigh, she sets the black box on the coffee table and tucks her feet beneath her. "A few different reasons. We hardly ever see each other," she admits. "But mostly because when I look at you and

Fallon, I know that's what I want to find. And, right now, it's not what I have."

For a moment, I'm not sure what to say. "Um, I hate to be the bearer of bad news, but Fallon's been running away from me since the moment we met."

"Not really, though. The way you two look at each other when you think no one is paying attention..." She sighs dreamily. "I want that."

"Do you think I actually have a shot with her?"

"Ryan, you're flipping hot. You could be with any woman you want. Including me."

I flush and she winks at me.

"But I know you're taken and I'm really happy for you both. You balance each other out in this really cool way."

"You'll find your man, Sierra. You're a sweetheart and I'm glad we've become friends."

A commotion fills the hall and Maddox stomps into the room, Sailor on his heels. "Stop running away from me, you stubborn ass," Sailor says in a frustrated voice.

"For someone who supposedly doesn't swear, she

sure does when he's around," I say under my breath and Sierra giggles.

They continue fighting as though we aren't even there.

"I said I'm fine," Maddox snaps. "Stop fawning all over me."

"You have a bump the size of a watermelon on the back of your head."

"A watermelon? Really?"

"Okay, more like a grapefruit. But that doesn't make it any less serious. You need to keep this cool compress on it and you aren't allowed to go to sleep yet. Not until we have the doctor check you out."

"I don't do doctors," he growls.

Sailor scowls at him fiercely, holding the washcloth out. With a grunt, he finally snatches it from her and holds it against the back of his head. "There. Happy?"

While they glare at each other, Eden and Fallon walk into the room. "Everything's all taken care of," Fallon announces.

"The bad guys are part of a local ring of thieves,"

Eden says. "They've had their eye on Cupid's Bow for months. When Sierra told the entire world over social media that her prince was gifting something to her, they took notice. It didn't help that she wrote #hopeitsjewelry and #rubiesareforever."

"That's really not something you should announce to the world," Sailor says, eyes on Maddox. When the washcloth slips too low, she pushes it back up and holds it in place, her fingers brushing his. Neither readjusts.

"I was excited," Sierra says with a shrug. "But now that the thieves have been caught, I don't think I'm going to need you to escort me back to New York, Fallon."

Fallon nods. "I think you're safe, but I'm available if you change your mind."

"Thanks, but I'll be fine. I'm sure there's a better way you can spend your time." She glances from Fallon over to me in a very obvious way.

"Well, if this is a wrap, I need to get back down to the office," Eden says. "I've been letting my paperwork build up again."

"Dash is going to kill you," Fallon says.

"Unless maybe you want to do it for me?"

"Hell no."

"You're always trying to pawn your paperwork off," Maddox grumbles.

"Because I'm all about the action, not the grunt work. Alright, let's head out," Eden says. "I'm driving. Sai, you can fawn over Maddox in the back."

Sailor's mouth drops open and Maddox mumbles a curse. I wonder how long they're going to keep playing games. Their chemistry is palpable and I'm willing to bet they'll crumble soon. *I have my own girl to worry about, though,* I think, and turn to Fallon.

"You're staying a little longer, right?" I ask and she nods. Releasing an internal sigh of relief, I turn to Fallon's team. "Thanks for having our backs."

"Any time," Eden says.

"It's just what we do," Sailor chimes in and Maddox gives a sharp nod.

Fallon hugs them all and they head out to the Range Rover.

"I'm sure we'll be seeing you later, Ryan," Eden says over her shoulder.

Will they? I wonder. *Damn, I hope so.*

"I'm going to stay here," Sierra announces. "Armand will be getting in tomorrow and it's best if I break things off in person."

"Good luck," Fallon says.

"Thank you for everything, Fallon." Sierra throws her arms around Fallon and hugs her. "If I ever need a bodyguard again, I'm calling you. Well, I'll want to talk to Dash first. My God, that man has a voice. All smooth and deep. A voice like that was made to whisper dirty things in a woman's ear all night."

"Goodbye, Sierra," Fallon says and I chuckle.

"Take care, Sierra." I give her a quick hug, mindful of Fallon waiting for me.

"You're amazing, Ryan. Now go get your girl," she adds in a low voice and we exchange conspiratorial looks.

Once we're outside, my nerves soar and I shift. I told Fallon I was falling in love with her and I have no idea how she's feeling. Granted I was a little drugged up at the time, but it was definitely the truth.

"I figure we can wrap things up at the safehouse and leave in the morning," she says.

"Okay," I say slowly. There are so many things I want to say, but I know I need to take this slowly. Tonight will either go extremely well or Fallon is going to bolt for good.

On the Uber drive back to Burbank, I start getting in my head and doubts begin creeping in. *What if Fallon decides she doesn't want me?*

There's no use pretending– I'm going to be fucking heartbroken.

We head into the house and I lock the door and slouch against it. My mind is going a million miles a minute and it's getting late fast. While I'm trying to figure out how to hang onto this amazing woman, Fallon reaches for my hand and tugs me forward.

"Where are we going?" I ask.

"I'm going to take a shower," she says and guides me down to her room. She pauses and gives me a small smile. "I was hoping you'd join me."

My mouth drops open and I snap it shut.

"Do you know how cute you are?" she asks and

starts getting undressed.

In my mind, cute equals geek.

She tosses her shirt and pauses. "What's wrong?"

"Cute?"

She must sense I'm not happy with her word choice because she thinks for a moment before saying, "Cute as in adorable. But you're so much more than that." She slides her hand around and squeezes my ass. "You're also really damn hot."

I watch her sashay over to the bathroom, shedding the rest of her clothes, and my mouth goes dry.

Damn hot works for me, I think, and whip my shirt off. I'm dying to touch her and follow her into the adjoining bathroom, quickly tearing off my jeans and boxers. Her body is tall, lithe and powerful. Fallon turns the shower on and steps inside. It's a roomy, walk-in setup with a built-in bench. She moves beneath the falling water and slicks her hair back.

For a moment, I stand there and watch the water sluice down her smooth skin. She's so damn beautiful and, even though my dick is urging me to get in, I hesitate. Whatever's happening between us…I need to make sure we're on the same page.

Fallon glances over at me and arches a dark brow. "Aren't you coming in?" Her gaze lowers and desire makes me grow and swell even more.

"I've never wanted a woman as much as I want you," I admit, voice low and husky. She licks the water off her lips and my nostrils flare. *Christ.* "I want you. All of you."

"So come here and take me."

I step in, moving under the spray and slide my arms around her waist, hauling her backside against me. My head drops to her neck and I kiss the wet skin, swirling my tongue and lapping up water droplets. She moans, leaning back, her head dropping against my shoulder.

"I want your trust," I rasp, hand sliding up to round over her full breast. She presses her ass further into my groin, rotating her hips, as my fingers play with a tight, rosy-tipped nipple. "Ah, Jesus," I murmur, my other hand moving down between her legs.

My fingers slide between her wet folds, teasing and stroking until she's bucking against my hand. She's so close and I keep doing exactly what I'm doing, not changing up a thing. "Let go," I whisper.

"Just for me." A moment later, she cries out and a series of shudders run through her body before she sags in my arms.

When Fallon gives up control and releases her inhibitions, it's breathtaking. I turn her around, backing her up, and place my palms on the cool tiles on either side of her. My head dips and captures her lips in a slow, possessive kiss. I want her to know how much I desire her. At some point, it became more than just physical.

I need this woman on every level.

Fallon pulls her mouth free and begins dropping kisses across my chest. Her soft lips and tongue trail lower and when I look down, she's on her knees. The moment her hands wrap around my straining dick, a deep groan rips from my throat.

I'm not expecting anything more so when her soft lips touch my engorged tip, the sweetest shock grips me. I reach down and caress a hand along her cheek. Her blue-green eyes lift to meet mine and I'm hovering on the edge of exquisite pleasure.

Even though my body is dying to feel her lips wrap around me, I slide my fingers through her wet hair, gently cupping the back of her head. "You don't have to," I rasp.

"I know," she says. "I want to. If that's okay?"

"Fuck yeah, it's more than okay," I manage to say. I'm not sure how I even get the words out with her hands sliding up and down my rigid shaft like they are, but after I say them, her mouth closes over my dick, sucking me deep and my eyes slide shut.

Colorful lights explode behind my eyelids and my hips rock but I let her control everything. My chest is heaving hard and I'm not sure how much longer I can take this kind of pleasure. Her mouth and hands are propelling me straight to a fucking powerful climax.

"Fallon," I groan, teetering on the edge.

Caught in a sensual haze, I grasp her shoulders and pull her up onto her feet. My hands slide around her waist and drop to cup her ass. I scoop her up and Fallon wraps her legs around me, lifting her hips, and positioning herself just right. She lowers herself down as I thrust up and we both groan as our bodies come together.

More fireworks burst behind my eyes and the need to possess this woman, *my* woman, fills me to the breaking point. I hope she's holding on because I've lost all control. I slam into her slick body, hard and fast, driving us toward the edge.

Fallon must be feeling the same overwhelming passion because she's riding me like a wild woman, nails digging into my biceps, and her soft cries echo all around us. When we both break a moment later, it's like a Fourth of July finale.

Fucking fantastic.

Afterward, coming down from the high, I feel a tremble run through her. I shut the water off, grab a towel and drape it around her. She's clinging to me like saran wrap, panting in my ear, and I walk into the bedroom. Her grip doesn't loosen, so I carefully lay down on the bed with her, tucking her against my body and pulling the sheet up.

I press a kiss into her damp hair and tighten my arms around her. *Yeah, no doubt about it.*

I love this woman.

Chapter Nineteen: Fallon

What just happened between us in the shower is more than I can wrap my mind around right now. It was so much more than just sex. It was a revelation.

I know Ryan Mercer is my person, the right man for me, and instead of running, I'm going to face the fact head-on and embrace it. The only way to do that is to confront my own feelings, and that's not easy for me.

All my life, I've been trying to be one of the guys; fighting to prove my worth. It's been my ultimate goal to show everyone how tough and strong I am. But Ryan taught me that it's also okay to be one of the girls. To embrace my soft and vulnerable side.

Because having those traits doesn't mean I'm weak. Only human.

It's probably why I love makeup so much. Allowing myself that bit of girliness makes me feel feminine and, after spending so much of my life surrounded by men and endless testosterone, it's something I need.

I want a future with this man. More than I've ever wanted anything in my entire life. But fear nips at me, makes me wary. I've lost the people I love most and I couldn't survive it again.

Snuggling down into Ryan's arms, I try to remain calm and not let panic consume me. Confiding my feelings is going to leave me raw and vulnerable. Open to potential heartbreak if he's not on the same page.

But I remember his words clearly:

"I could live on the moon and it wouldn't matter. Wherever you are is where I belong."

"How can you be so sure?"

"Because I'm falling in love with you."

"Ryan-"

"No. Don't say anything. Not yet."

It's time for me to say something and all I can do is chew on the inside of my lip and squeeze the sheet in my fist.

Shit. For someone who has always considered herself so brave, I feel like a coward.

"Fallon?" Ryan murmurs, lips near my ear.

"Hmm?"

"I want you to know you're safe with me. Whatever you say or do, it's only between us."

I release a pent-up breath and all the air rushes out of my lungs. "I know I'm not the easiest person to understand," I say, trying to sort through all of my confusing thoughts. "I've been through a lot and…I've built walls to protect myself."

His hand runs up and down my arm, soothing me, and I'm finding it easier to talk when I'm wrapped up in his embrace like this, facing the opposite direction.

"It's hard for you to open up," he says. "I get it."

"Incredibly hard," I admit. "But you make me want to try."

His hand stops moving and his body tenses behind me.

"Ryan?"

"Can you turn around?"

I let out a shaky breath and reluctantly turn to face him. His serious brown gaze sweeps my face and locks hold with mine.

"When I came out here, I had no real plans other than hanging out at the beach and going surfing."

"You surf?"

His mouth edges up. "I do. Not as often as I'd like but, yeah."

"You're always surprising me. Not many people do."

"There's a lot you don't know about me," he says and brushes my hair back.

"I'd like to learn more."

"I'm glad. Because meeting you and running from bad guys hasn't just been the highlight of my trip. It's been the highlight of my life."

My heart trips in my chest and I trace my index finger over his chest. A warmth fills me and the strange thing is I have no urge to bolt. "Really?" I manage to ask.

"Accidentally taking your suitcase was the best mistake I ever made."

"I was so mad at the time." I lift my hand and cup his face, enjoying the scratch of his stubble. "But you intrigued me from the first moment I saw you in your geeky t-shirt and sexy glasses."

"You think my glasses are sexy?" he asks, voice full of doubt.

"Oh, you have no idea. They're sexy as hell."

Ryan chuckles. "Interesting. I'll have to remember that."

"I have no doubt that you will," I tease, running my hand through his damp hair. "You stuck around and helped when you didn't have to– despite my occasional grumpiness– and I'm so grateful that you did."

"Why?" he asks, voice low, brown eyes searching mine.

I hesitate for a brief moment. "Because you're the best thing that's ever happened to me."

A smile lifts his mouth and I lean in to kiss him.

When we finally pull apart, a wave of shyness washes over me, but I know I have to tell him exactly how I'm feeling.

"There's more," I say. He waits patiently for me to gather my thoughts. "Other than my Slater Security family, I haven't had anyone in my life that I care about."

"Do you have any family left?"

I swallow hard and shake my head. Talking about what happened when I was 16 isn't something I do. Ever. The only other person in this whole world who knows the truth is Dash, and I only confided the story of my parents' death because we were cornered in some shithole in the Middle East and I thought we were going to die. Other than him, I've never told a soul. "I lost my parents when I was 16," I say. The tremble in my voice makes me pause.

"I'm so sorry, Fallon."

I nod and look down to see him lace his long fingers through mine. "We were driving back home after visiting their friends up at the lake. My dad stopped to get gas and-"

"You're okay," he murmurs.

My anchor, I think. Ryan makes me feel so secure and I continue the story. "Some asshole robber stormed in, waving a gun around, and he was high. He shot the cashier and then he-" My voice cracks and I squeeze his hand hard. "He killed my dad and then my mom."

"Jesus."

"I remember standing there, looking down the barrel of his gun, and not knowing if I was going to be next. I can still see their blood all over the floor. Splattered on fucking bags of chips." My eyes prick with tears. "For whatever reason, he didn't shoot me and instead went around the counter. He started banging his fist on the register, trying to open it. I was frozen and couldn't move. My dad was in front of me on the floor and I could just see my mom's legs. But I knew they were both gone."

When I finally find the courage to look into his dark eyes, it's not sympathy I see.

It's compassion and love. And so much support. He's providing a solid foundation to help prop me up when I could curl up and cry.

"What happened?"

"A man came in and he was carrying. He shot the

robber dead without even blinking. I later learned his name was Sam and he was former military. He probably saved my life."

Ryan lets out an unsteady breath. "You're so damn lucky he showed up when he did."

"You just never know when you're going to be in the wrong place at the wrong time. But I knew that if there was a next time, I'd be prepared. After that day, I promised myself I would never be a victim again. The moment I turned 18, I signed up for the Army and never looked back. I wanted to be able to protect myself and others. Like Sam."

"Fuck," he says and pulls me close. "I can't even begin to imagine what that must've been like for you and I'm so sorry you had to go through that."

"It's strange because even though it was so long ago, sometimes it feels like yesterday. And the nightmares don't help. They've never completely gone away."

He presses his cheek against my hair. "That night you woke up…" Understanding fills his voice. "Shit. I wish I'd known."

"That night, I dreamed the entire thing from beginning to end and it felt like it had just happened all over again. That's why I was such a damn mess. I hadn't broken down like that since the day it happened."

"Oh, baby," he murmurs and places a kiss against my temple. "If I could take it away, I would."

"I know. It's weird that the thing that almost broke me actually made me stronger and gave me a reason to work so hard. When I joined the Army, I didn't hold back. I threw myself into everything and vowed to climb as high as I could. Other than becoming a Navy SEAL, Delta Force was the toughest, hardest, baddest thing I could accomplish. And when I set my mind on something, I do everything in my power to accomplish it."

"You should be so proud of yourself."

I shrug a shoulder. "It was a job and I became damn good at it. That's how I met Dash– he was my commander. We've been through a lot of shit together. After separating from the military, I felt lost until he called and offered me a job at his new security company."

"Is there anything more between you two?" Ryan asks carefully.

"Me and Dash?" I shake my head. "He's like a

bossy, older brother. Some days I want to kill him, but we're family and I love him. Just not in the romantic sense."

"Gotta say I'm a little relieved. I'm not sure I could compete with a former Delta Force commander with cheeks that could cut glass. According to Sierra, anyway."

I burst out laughing. "You have nothing to worry about, Mercer." I turn my head and press a kiss to his jaw.

"No?"

"Nope. It seems that you're the one I've fallen in love with," I say.

His dark eyes light up. "Oh, really?"

"I should probably warn you– I've never been in love with anyone before and I have no idea how to have a serious relationship."

"We'll figure it out together," he murmurs and pulls me in for a long, slow kiss that sends a shiver down my spine. When we finally come up for air, Ryan cups my face and traces a finger over my lower lip. "I love you, Fallon."

"I love you, too," I whisper. It's not as hard to say as I thought it would be. In fact, I like saying those words to Ryan. A lot.

We end up making love again, a phrase I've never used in my life, but that's exactly what it is– a mind-blowing physical and emotional connection that is so much more than sex. Afterward, we share a pillow, facing each other, and I can't help but think about our current dilemma.

"We live on opposite sides of the country," I say, stroking a hand over his hard bicep.

"Fallon, wherever you are is where I plan to be."

"Really? Would you move to San Diego?"

"Baby, I'd move to the moon for you."

"You did mention that." Emotion makes my heart swell. "You're so sweet. I'm not used to that."

"Well, get used to it because I'm going to treat you like a princess. Whatever you want, just tell me."

"There is something, actually."

"What?"

"It sounds silly, but I'd like a kitchen table," I

say.

That must be the last thing he expects me to say, but his mouth curves up in a smile. "Okay. You need a new one?"

I shake my head. "I've never had one. I just sit on my couch and eat at my coffee table. It's always just been me."

"Not anymore," Ryan says. "I'll get you the biggest, fanciest table at the store."

I lay a hand over his heart, feeling its strong, steady beat.

"I want you to come down to San Diego with me in the morning. Check it out and see what you think."

"I already love it," he assures me. "Because I love you." He slides his hand through my hair to cup the back of my neck and then we kiss.

We kiss and kiss and then kiss some more.

******

The next morning, Ryan and I take an Uber over to the airport right up the street. The private jet that brought Eden and Sailor up waits on the tarmac.

"There's our ride," I say and wave to Eric Finn, one of Dash's pilots. "Eric Finn, this is Ryan Mercer."

They shake hands. "Nice to meet you. And just call me Finn, pilot extraordinaire."

I roll my eyes. *Typical cocky flyboy.* "Finn is former spec ops if you haven't already guessed. He was a Night Stalker."

Finn winks at me. "Don't be jealous that I got to fly while you had boots on the ground."

We climb up and get settled. It's a quick, easy flight and it seems like we're landing a few minutes later. Finn opens the door and walks us out. He's giving me a funny look and when we hit the tarmac, I pause.

"What?" I ask and place a hand on my hip.

"Never thought I'd see the day," Finn says.

"What're you talking about?"

"Fallon Pierce in love. I'm happy for you." Before I can comment, he gives me a hug and claps a hand on the back of Ryan's shoulder. "You do know her nickname, right?"

Ryan's mouth edges up. "I hear it's Dangerous.

But I refer to her as Boss."

Finn laughs. "Even better."

We say goodbye and roll our suitcases over to the Range Rover Eden and Sailor parked in the hangar for us. It doesn't take long to get to the Slater Security office and when we walk inside, Ryan looks over the sleek leather furniture and fancy paintings hanging on the walls. It's clean and modern with plenty of light streaming in through large floor to ceiling windows.

"Hey, girl. Welcome back," Sailor says, walking over. Her blonde hair is up in a high ponytail and she blows a bubble. "Hi, Ryan."

"Hi, Sailor," Ryan says.

"Is Dash in his office?" I ask.

"Sure is. Oh, and guess who's asleep in the other holding cell downstairs?"

"Who?"

"Blue Eyes. He's been interrogating Veronica for five days straight now. Dash finally convinced him to lay down and he's been out for almost three hours. Even though he's asleep, he doesn't look any less intense."

"I'm not surprised."

"I called Oz and said he should probably come pick him up."

"Good idea."

"Who are Oz and Blue Eyes?" Ryan asks.

"Jack Cullen and Aidan Wolf, former SEALs. It's a long story," I say wearily and nod toward Dash's office. "C'mon."

When we reach the big corner office, I knock on the door and step inside. Dash sits at a large walnut desk and looks up from his laptop. As usual, he wears a navy blue suit and is much more reserved and buttoned-up than the rest of us.

"Welcome back," Dash says and stands up. "You must be Ryan."

"Nice to meet you. I've heard a lot about you."

Dash scrapes a hand over his clean-shaven jaw. "From this one?" he asks and glances at me. "I'm not sure if that's good or bad."

"Would I bad mouth you?" I ask, all innocence.

He makes a scoffing sound and sits on the edge

of his desk. "Depends on what day of the week it is," Dash says with a crooked grin.

Even though I have zero romantic interest in the man, I guess I can see why Sierra and other women find him so attractive. He's tall with a lean build and has a head of thick, dark hair that reaches the edge of his collar. His teal eyes are ringed in a darker indigo blue and I suppose he does have a nice voice. I saw him in muddy fatigues for years and I'm still getting used to seeing him in a suit now. *Oh, yeah. And then there are the cheekbones.*

Despite their sharpness, Dash Slater will always be a brother to me.

"See what I have to deal with," I say as Ryan checks the place out.

"You have a nice setup here," Ryan comments. "How long have you been in business?"

"Almost three years. We're a small group but we're equipped to handle big jobs."

"No doubt," Ryan says. "I've met your team and seen them in action. They're impressive."

"We get it done."

"So, I'm not sure what the girls have told you," I begin tentatively. "But Ryan is moving out here. We're going to live together."

"They may have mentioned the two of you are desperately in love," Dash says, a teasing glow in his bright blue eyes.

My cheeks redden and Ryan reaches for my hand. "They'd be right," he says and we share a smile.

Dash studies us closely but keeps his expression neutral and guarded, as usual. He has the best poker face I've ever seen and reading him is nearly impossible. "I'm happy for you both," he says. "Surprised to see Fallon take the plunge, but I have a feeling you're going to be good for her."

"Maybe we can work on finding you a girlfriend next, Slater," I say with a teasing grin.

"Don't waste your time," he mutters.

"I'm sure there's a woman out there somewhere who will put up with your BS."

"Doubtful. Anyway," he says, swiftly changing the subject, "I hear you have a photographic memory."

Ryan nods. "Comes in handy every once in a

while."

"Like when you can remember a 20-digit combination made up of numbers, letters and symbols." Dash crosses his arms. "What are your job plans?"

Ryan glances at me in surprise and I give him an encouraging nod. Knowing Dash, he's going to try to scoop Ryan and his talents up. I had mentioned that he was into tech stuff and computers and we've been wanting to hire an IT person for months now.

"I was in the medical field but decided it wasn't for me. Since I've always been a tech geek at heart, I had plans to open my own IT company."

"What do you think about working here? As our tech guru?"

"Seriously?"

"If you're interested, we can talk salary. But we need someone who knows what to do when Maddox throws his computer across the room and crashes our entire system."

"Which he's managed to do twice," I say.

"Um, yeah, sure, I'm very interested. I mean, as

long as you don't mind me being here," Ryan says and turns toward me. "I don't want to crowd you or make you have to live and work with me if it's too much."

God, he's the sweetest. "Mercer, the more time I'm with you, the better." We share a kiss and Dash clears his throat.

"Great, it's settled then. After you're all moved in, come on by and we'll get you set up."

"Thank you," Ryan says and he and Dash shake hands.

I give Dash a grateful smile and then Ryan and I turn to leave.

"Oh, and Ryan? One more thing," Dash says, settling back behind his desk.

"What's that?"

"You hurt her and I'll hurt you." Dash's blue eyes flash as he steeples his fingers beneath his chin. "Welcome to the team."

"Thanks," Ryan murmurs and I tug him out the door with a chuckle. "Is he always so joyless and threatening?"

"Nah. Once you get to know him, you'll see he's

just a big pushover." I lace my fingers through his and we stop, turning to face each other. "What do you think? Are you ready to join the Slater Security team?"

"As long as I have you by my side, I'm ready for anything."

"Thank you, Ryan," I whisper and slide my hands up and around his neck.

"For what?"

"For loving me for exactly who I am."

"Always, boss," he promises.

When our lips meet, I feel that spark of excitement that had been missing for a very long time. There was an empty hole that I didn't know how to fill. But now I realize the hole was in my heart and Ryan has filled it with love.

After a long steamy kiss, I pull back and look up into Ryan's dark, espresso eyes and see the start of a whole new adventure.

And I've never been so excited.

I hope you enjoyed Fallon and Ryan's story! Up next, find out what happens when Eden collides with the one man from her past who she's never been able to forget.

You can grab "Operation: Shadow Catcher" here: https://mybook.to/OperationShadowCatcher

About the Author

A Midwest girl at heart, Charissa has lived in Boston and Los Angeles and finally returned to her hometown of Toledo, Ohio. She's an avid coffee drinker, animal lover and was named after a romance heroine. Horror movies and steamy, action-packed romance novels keep her up late at night (and probably too much caffeine). She's also written over 15 screenplays, several even produced, and despite a dreary dating history, she still believes in love at first sight.

Don't Miss Out!

To be notified of upcoming releases, news, sneak peeks and contests, come join my reading crew: https://www.facebook.com/groups/1506114033137424

And if you enjoy steamy romantic suspense, don't forget to claim your free story, "Blue Squadron Pirates," the prequel to Project Phoenix, here: https://BookHip.com/NLVKTAL

It's only available for readers who sign up for my VIP mailing list! You can sign up over at www.charissagracyk.com

If you love my stories and would like free advanced copies of my books, I'm still building my ARC team and would love to have you! Just message me on my Facebook page, Charissa Gracyk, Author, or at charissagracyk@gmail.com.

Also By Charissa Gracyk

Fortune Seekers

Brighter Than Gold (Fortune Seekers Book 1)

The Brilliance of You (Fortune Seekers Book 2)

Dazzled By You (Fortune Seekers Book 3)

A Million Sparks (Fortune Seekers Book 4)

**Each book in this steamy, action-packed, romantic adventure series can be read as a standalone.

Project Phoenix

Reactivated: Oz (Project Phoenix Book1)

Reactivated: Dom (Project Phoenix Book 2)

Reactivated: Jericho (Project Phoenix Book 3)

Reactivated: Max (Project Phoenix Book 4)

Reactivated: Cassian (Project Phoenix Book 5)

Reactivated: Deacon (Project Phoenix Book 6)

Reactivated: Aidan (Project Phoenix Book 7)

**This is an interconnected series and each warrior finds a happily-ever-after in his own story.

Slater Security

Operation: Dead Drop (Slater Security Book 1)

Operation: Shadow Catcher (Slater Security Book 2)

Operation: Light Storm (Slater Security Book 3)

Operation: Fire Bomb (Slater Security Book 4)

Operation: Free Fall (Slater Security Book 5)

**This is a spinoff of Project Phoenix but each book in this steamy, action-packed, romantic adventure series can be read as a standalone.

Made in the USA
Coppell, TX
26 September 2025